Justin i
him to a

The instant her body
blank, heat silencing his intended reprimand
to the hooligans. Elisabeth's sharp intake of
breath was audible and, from his view over
her shoulder, did mesmerizing things for her
cleavage.

She craned her head to look up at him.
"Thanks." The word ended on a near whisper
as their gazes locked. She was right there, so
close, in his arms the way she'd been hundreds
of times before. The urge to kiss her was so
natural....

"Justin?" Her voice was a squeak of uncertainty,
jarring him from lust-addled memories.

He immediately dropped his hands to his sides,
hoping he looked more innocent than he felt.
"Just wanted to make sure you didn't get hurt."

A hollow chuckle escaped her. "Ironic, coming
from you."

He flinched. "Guess I deserved that."

He took a step back, trying to repress the
desire he'd felt, trying to repress memories of
how exquisit   ys been
to his kisses

"I should go," she stammered.

Dear Reader,

When I wrote my first Colorado Cades book *(Her Secret, His Baby),* I knew I couldn't wait for the chance to give the heroine's brother Justin his own story.

Search-and-rescue patroller Justin Cade is many things—an excellent skier, a terrific big brother and an incorrigible charmer. But, after losing both his parents young, the one thing he *doesn't* do well is commitment. Seemingly carefree Justin refuses to get close and risk more pain, a lesson Elisabeth Donnelly learned all too well.

Now that Elisabeth has custody of her orphaned goddaughter, it's more important than ever to make smart decisions for the future. No more pining over blue-eyed heartbreakers! She's engaged to marry a man who is in many ways Justin's opposite. So why are fate and several meddlesome siblings determined to throw her and Justin together?

When her goddaughter goes missing in a blizzard, Elisabeth relies on Justin for help. But can she rely on him emotionally? Luckily, Christmas is the season of miracles....

If you enjoy Justin and Elisabeth's story, be sure to follow me on Twitter or like me on Facebook for updates on the next book in the Colorado Cades trilogy.

Happy holidays,

Tanya

SECOND CHANCE CHRISTMAS

TANYA MICHAELS

HARLEQUIN® AMERICAN ROMANCE®

Recycling programs
for this product may
not exist in your area.

ISBN-13: 978-0-373-75483-0

SECOND CHANCE CHRISTMAS

Printed in U.S.A.

www.Harlequin.com

ABOUT THE AUTHOR

New York Times bestselling author and three-time RITA® Award nominee Tanya Michaels writes about what she knows—community, family and lasting love! Her books, praised for their poignancy and humor, have received honors such as a Booksellers' Best Bet Award, a Maggie Award of Excellence and multiple readers' choice awards. She was also a 2010 *RT Book Reviews* nominee for Career Achievement in Category Romance. Tanya is an active member of Romance Writers of America and a frequent public speaker, presenting workshops to educate and encourage aspiring writers. She lives outside Atlanta with her very supportive husband, two highly imaginative children and a household of quirky pets, including a cat who thinks she's a dog and a bichon frise who thinks she's the center of the universe.

Books by Tanya Michaels

HARLEQUIN AMERICAN ROMANCE

For Sally Kilpatrick—my gratitude goes beyond words. Fully expressing my thanks may require interpretative dance and puppetry.

Chapter One

Justin Cade's specialty was women. While his colleagues on rescue patrol could attest he was a remarkably skilled skier, it was his expertise with females that made him infamous throughout Cielo Peak, Colorado. He may have set a town record with the number of women he'd dated, but he also used his powers for good. When a neighbor had been hell-bent on running over her unfaithful husband, it was Justin who'd charmed her into relinquishing her car keys. Over the summer, when his sister, Arden, had been in the clutches of pregnancy mood swings, it was Justin who'd had the most success calming her.

So when he heard an outraged female shriek, "Justin Cade, you heartless ass!" across the sporting goods shop, he wasn't too worried. His first reaction was gratitude that she'd momentarily drowned out the incessant Christmas music. Retailers had barely waited for Halloween to pass before bombarding shoppers with holiday tunes. There were still two weeks before Christmas, but Justin had hit his limit on *fa-la-las* and *rum-pa-pum-pums*.

Preparing to face his accuser, he turned from the

shelf of ski wax, a conciliatory smile in place. It faltered when he caught a glimpse of red hair. *Elisabeth?* Conflicting feelings swirled through him, and his pulse had already accelerated in the split second it took him to realize his mistake. It wasn't Elisabeth Donnelly. Stupid to think it might have been—she was far too poised to shout across a store.

No, it was her twin sister, Evangeline, better known as Lina, barreling toward him. *What did I do to rile her?* When it came to the Donnellys, he'd tried to keep a low profile since breaking up with Elisabeth five months ago.

Lina skipped the traditional "hello" in favor of threatening him. "If I weren't a foot shorter than you, I'd tear you limb from limb. It's kismet, running into you after what I learned this morning. The universe wants you to know this is *your fault*."

He ducked his head in agreement. "You're probably right. Unfortunately, my sins are so numerous, I'm not sure which one you mean."

"Elisabeth." Her voice was ice. "You remember her, don't you?"

Vividly.

The Donnelly twins, though they shared the same height and build, were not identical. Impulsive Lina, with her strawberry-blond ponytail, was cute. Elisabeth was striking. Her hair was a deeper red, cut in a silky bob that perfectly framed her features and moss-green eyes. Because Lina was more outspoken, people considered her the more fiery of the two. Anyone foolish enough to believe that had never kissed Elisabeth. She'd been like live flame in his arms.

He cleared his throat. "What about your sister? Is she okay?"

"No, she's lost her ever-loving mind! She told us over brunch that she and Kaylee…" Lina trailed off, blinking furiously. "They're leaving Cielo Peak. And I blame you."

Leaving? But Elisabeth had spent her entire life here. She helped run the family-owned Donnelly Ski Lodge. Her father had been grooming her to take over since she was a teenager. And Justin couldn't imagine her uprooting Kaylee Truitt. He'd only met Elisabeth's goddaughter a handful of times, but even he understood how traumatic the past year had been for the little girl.

"Are you sure they're leaving?" he asked. "Maybe you mis—"

"Would I be this upset if I wasn't sure?"

He still didn't see what this had to do with him, but he reluctantly empathized with her agitation. Justin's own sister was preparing to move away, and he hadn't seen his older brother in over a month. Soon, Justin would be alone.

Shaking off that melancholy thought, he refocused on Lina. "I know you'll miss her. The two of you have always been close, but—"

"Spare me the faux sensitivity! I don't want sympathy from someone who acts like people are disposable. You have a different woman on your arm every week."

"Be that as it may," he countered in a low, tight voice, "I know a little something about losing family." He hadn't meant to say anything so personal. This damn season was getting to him. If time healed all wounds, why wasn't December ever any easier?

"I'm sorry. I forgot about your sister-in-law's crash." Lina's pale cheeks flushed with shame. "And your parents—"

"Died a long time ago. No need to dredge it up now." He couldn't. He couldn't stand in the middle of the store and discuss his mom and dad with a casual acquaintance while some ridiculous song about wanting a hippopotamus for Christmas played overhead. With effort, he relaxed his clenched jaw. "If you'll excuse me, I'm going to make my purchase and forget this charming encounter ever took place."

He grabbed a container of ski wax and moved to pass her.

She touched his arm. "Elisabeth is about to make the biggest mistake of her life."

What did Lina expect him to do? Justin could barely be trusted to handle his own life. He shrugged. "Maybe she needs a temporary change of pace. It doesn't have to be a permanent, forever-and-ever decision."

"Actually...we aren't just talking about a change of scenery. It's way worse. Being on the rebound from you made my normally brilliant sister stupid."

Not possible. Elisabeth was the sharpest person he knew. She had a mind like a computer.

"After you broke her heart," Lina continued, "she met a software developer from Albuquerque. Justin, she's getting married."

Am I doing this wrong? It was a question Elisabeth Donnelly had begun asking herself daily since becoming guardian to her six-year-old goddaughter. Despite the months that had passed, there were still moments she couldn't believe she was a parent, couldn't believe that her friend and former college roommate, Michelle, was gone.

Right now, Kaylee was staring back across the kitchen table with brown eyes that were exactly like her late mother's. From her curly dark hair to her freckles, the kindergartener was a mini-Michelle. Similarities between mother and daughter weren't just physical, either. They had being orphaned in common. Former foster child Michelle Truitt had gone to college on a state scholarship and had no known relatives. She'd been a single mom. Elisabeth couldn't predict how Kaylee would feel about having a father figure for the first time in her life.

"You understand everything I'm telling you?" Elisabeth asked cautiously. Earlier that Sunday, while Kaylee had gone with a classmate to a holiday puppet show, Elisabeth had taken the opportunity to tell her parents and sister about her engagement. Their reactions had been immediate and dramatic. In comparison, Kaylee's unblinking expression revealed nothing.

The little girl nodded. "You're marrying Mr. Steven. We're all gonna live together."

"Right. But you don't have to say 'mister,' honey. You can just say *Steven,* like you do *Elisabeth.*" At the funeral, her heart had squeezed into a painful knot when Kaylee asked between sobs, "Do I hafta call you Mommy now?" Elisabeth had blurted *no* so quickly she'd worried about making the child feel unwanted. To soften the refusal, she'd clarified that it was Kaylee's choice.

Choices. Since August, it felt as if Elisabeth had

been constantly second-guessing hers. While she'd never been as brashly confident as her sister, the former prom queen, Elisabeth had been sure of herself in other, less outspoken ways. That steady self-assurance had been shaken by the one-two punch of the man she loved dumping her and being thrust a few weeks later into parenthood. Now there was a small person in her life who was wholly dependent on her, who would be impacted by every decision Elisabeth made.

Then I'd better make the right ones. "Do you like Steven?" she prompted.

Kaylee's only answer was a barely perceptible shrug of her slim shoulders.

Oh, dear. "The two of you seemed to have fun at the zoo yesterday."

The girl didn't do anything so radical as smile, but her gaze brightened fractionally. "Monkeys are funny." Then she shoved an entire cookie into her mouth. Was that her way of ending the conversation?

Sighing, Elisabeth told herself that Steven and Kaylee would have plenty of time to bond. At least they'd met now. Since nearly all of Elisabeth and Steven's relationship had been long-distance, she'd refused to answer his proposal until he'd spent a couple of days with Kaylee. Elisabeth had pulled Kaylee from school early on Thursday and taken her to Albuquerque. By the time they'd arrived back home this morning, Elisabeth was officially engaged.

She'd wanted her parents and sister to hear the announcement first so they had time to work through their—*misgivings*—surprise and could help bolster Kaylee's enthusiasm. That plan might not work as well as she'd hoped. Lina had looked downright betrayed by Elisabeth's news, but surely she would remain positive in front of Kaylee? Over the past four months, Lina had proven herself a natural-born aunt.

An aunt who's about to be nine hundred miles from her niece. Elisabeth and Steven wanted to get married before his upcoming promotion took him to California. Moving to neutral ground together, as a family, would give them the perfect fresh start. He'd suggested that after he got settled into his new job, they could take Kaylee to Disneyland.

Elisabeth debated whether mention of Disney would perk up the little girl, but decided to keep that as an ace in her sleeve. "Are you all done with the cookies Chef made you?" A surprising bond had formed between Kaylee and the lodge's award-winning Chef Bates. Just that morning he'd delivered a small box of jelly-frosted spice cookies.

Kaylee nodded solemnly. "Can I go play?"

"Yes, but I'm here if you want to talk. About anything," she encouraged. "Even monkeys."

Her goddaughter silently slid from her chair and darted for freedom—only to retrace her steps and grab one last cookie before disappearing around the corner. Elisabeth didn't have the heart to call her back and remind her to take a napkin. After moving from Denver to Cielo Peak earlier in the year and finally beginning to adapt, poor Kaylee was about to be shifted again. She'd earned the right to scatter a few crumbs through Elisabeth's loft apartment.

Cookies and monkeys—I can do this. She'd made a promise to Michelle. Whatever it took, Elisabeth would raise a happy, well-adjusted daughter. But she was indescribably grateful that she would be married soon and wouldn't have to do it alone.

Chapter Two

While tourists usually congregated in the surrounding resort bars, Cielo Peak locals favored Peak's Pints. Especially on Tuesday nights, when pitchers of beer were only a dollar. Elisabeth scanned the crowded tavern for a free table. At least she had plenty of illumination for her search. The usual neon signs were supplemented by Christmas lights strewn all around the interior.

Her attention snagged on the cheerfully crooked Christmas tree next to the jukebox. Between extra hours during the lodge's busy holiday season and her weekend trip to New Mexico, she hadn't put up a tree yet. Would decorating one be fun for Kaylee, or would it simply remind the girl that she was facing her first Christmas without her mother?

"Hey!" Lina elbowed her in the side. "We're here to celebrate, not stand in the doorway all night."

"I'm looking for a place to sit. It's packed. You see anything, Nic?"

Boutique owner Nicole Lewis had the best vantage point. While the Donnelly twins barely topped five foot three, Nicole was almost six feet tall. With her natural grace and high cheekbones, she looked more like someone who modeled clothes on a runway than someone who sold them.

"Back corner, follow me." Wasting no time, Nicole strode in that direction.

They all hurried, hoping to secure the spot before anyone else took it, but they hadn't gone far when a man rose from his chair to hug Lina. Lifelong experience had taught Elisabeth that her twin would probably pause to say hi to a half dozen more people along the way. Elisabeth continued on without her.

Shrugging out of her coat, she slid into the booth across from Nicole. Although her friend had only moved here four years ago, Elisabeth often felt as if they'd known each other their whole lives. "I know I said this over the phone already, but that's not the same as face-to-face. Thank you for agreeing to be my maid of honor. The wedding plans are moving fast, and I really appreciate the help."

"I'm flattered you asked me. But surprised you didn't pick Lina."

"Well, she'll be a bridesmaid, of course. I know I can count on you. You have good attention to detail. Lina…" Elisabeth chose her words carefully. "…favors spontaneity."

"Says the woman who shocked us all with her engagement," Nicole teased.

"I admit the timing might seem sudden, but with Steven relocating to California in six weeks, taking this step now is logical."

"I think you've said 'logical' ten times since you called me about the engagement." Nicole propped her chin on her fist. "Know what I haven't heard you say? Romantic. Passionate."

Elisabeth grimaced. "I've had my share of passion."

"You mean Justin Cade?" Even Nicole, the most loyal of friends, sounded a bit breathless when she mentioned Mr. Tall, Dark and Temporary. Where Justin was concerned, women easily lost their breath. And their good sense. And often their clothes.

"Right. That guy."

"I never expected you to get over him so soon. Not to poke at emotional wounds, but you seemed destroyed when the two of you broke up over the summer."

"I don't like to dwell on that." The memory of herself as fragile and weepy embarrassed her. She was a strong, intelligent woman, someone who was supposed to be a role model for Kaylee. "It's been plenty of time to get over a guy—even one who thinks he's God's gift to women."

Nicole looked unconvinced. "We're talking about more than simple recovery after an ex. In less than six months, you healed your heartbreak, fell for someone else *and* decided to get married."

"Steven and I have spent a lot of hours Skyping. You know how upset I was when Michelle died, and he was such an incredible listener. We've gotten to know each other, discussed our goals for the future. We're not rushing into this blindly." Since most of their relationship had been conducted long-distance, they'd skipped banal courting activities such as sitting through two-hour movies without speaking or dancing at clubs where they couldn't hear each other over the music. Their time had been brief but effectively utilized. It was like the industrial-strength laundry detergent used by the lodge's housekeeping staff—one didn't need as much because it was so concentrated. "Why waste time when we both know what we want?"

"If you're happy, then I'm thrilled for you. Truly. But I'll miss you like crazy."

Elisabeth blinked, feeling a burn in her throat that she hoped didn't make it to her eyes. "Me, too." Unlike her life-of-the-party sister who had a seemingly endless stream of casual buddies, Elisabeth's friendships were generally limited to one or two people she trusted implicitly. How long would it take her to build new relationships?

They were interrupted by the waitress, who took their order for a pitcher and an appetizer sampler.

"If Lina doesn't get here soon," Elisabeth said, "I'm eating her share of the food." She glanced back in the direction where she'd last seen her sister, then stiffened when she saw a familiar foursome of men.

"Something wrong?" Nicole followed her gaze until she, too, spotted Justin. "Oh. Speak of the devil."

"In this case, literally." Elisabeth scouted for the waitress—that cold beer couldn't get here soon enough. "No matter. It's a small town. Run-ins are inevitable in Cielo Peak."

"But not in California."

"What's that sup—"

"Sorry I took so long," Lina burbled, handing her purse and jacket to Nicole to add to the pile next to her. "Did I miss anything?"

"No," Elisabeth said firmly. "I was just about to tell

Nicole that I can't wait for you both to meet Steven. He gets in Thursday night."

He was spending a long weekend with her family before leaving to have Christmas with his folks. It would probably be the last holiday they each spent with their respective families.

"Looking forward to it," Nicole said. She widened her smile to near-manic proportions, no doubt to make up for Lina's marked silence.

Elisabeth was getting frustrated by her family's lack of support. She knew this move wasn't quite what they wanted for her, but these were the same people who had hinted she should settle down and have beautiful babies with Justin Cade. Clearly their judgment was flawed. Justin was never going to settle down. Instead of pining for the wickedly charming ski patroller with his piercing aquamarine eyes, Elisabeth had met a successful man with no commitment phobias.

"Definite progress," she muttered.

"What about progress?" Lina asked.

Heat flooded Elisabeth's face. She hadn't meant to voice her thoughts, but she seized the moment anyway. "*I'm* making progress," she said proudly. "My taste in men demonstrates personal growth. Steven is several evolutionary steps above my last boyfriend."

When it looked as if Lina might protest, Nicole interjected, "We're behind you one hundred percent. If your heart tells you Steven's The One, then I'm sure you're right."

Elisabeth gave her friend a grateful smile even as she secretly rejected the sentiment. Follow her heart? No. She'd merrily tripped down that path before, smacking into an abrupt dead end. This time she was trusting her intellect.

Hadn't her parents and teachers told her for years that her keen mind was her strongest asset? Smart people learned from their mistakes, and that's precisely what Justin had been. A colossal mistake.

JUSTIN WAS NOT, by nature, maudlin or introspective— he preferred adjectives like *fun* and *uncomplicated.* But this year's annual December gloom seemed even worse than in past years. Joining a few of his off duty search-and-rescue colleagues for a pitcher of beer might be just what he needed.

It looked like standing room only tonight. Apparently, a few teenagers had hoped that, in the chaos, they could slip in with fake IDs. Shaking his head, Justin watched as they were escorted to the back room, where the owner would call their parents. Dumb kids. They should have gone one county over where they wouldn't have been recognized, the way he'd done at nineteen.

Trey Grainger, the oldest in Justin's party, was shaking his head for other reasons. "How can anyone stand the volume in here? The noise is shattering my brain cells."

Justin was glad for the buzz of boisterous conversation. If there was Christmas music playing, it was obliterated by the decibel level.

Chris Hyatt smirked at Trey. "If you don't like the volume, you should have left your hearing aid in the truck with your cane. Problem solved."

Trey was only forty, but Hyatt, all of twenty-three,

constantly needled him about his age. Trey's habitual response was to sock the rookie in the shoulder. Hard.

Tonight, Nate Washington responded before Trey could. He smacked Hyatt on the side of his blond head. "Don't you know to respect your elders, son?" His eyes twinkled as he added, "How would you like it if some whippersnapper talked to *your* grandpa the way you do to Grainger?"

"Hey!" Trey objected. "I'm not anyone's grandfather, and you damn well know it."

Justin ignored the familiar banter while he searched for a place to sit. His group caught the gaze of Mr. Merriweather, a man who'd injured himself on a ski trail last winter. Nate and Trey had given him on-the-spot medical attention. Mr. Merriweather waved the patrollers over to the U-shaped booth he shared with his wife and another couple.

Mr. Merriweather rose from the booth. "We were just leaving. I insist you boys take our seats." He pulled a dollar from his wallet. "Have a round on me."

Nate thanked the man and reminded him to always ski with protective gear and well-maintained equipment. All four patrollers sat, with Justin and Trey on the ends. Justin was glancing around for a waitress when his gaze landed unerringly on Elisabeth Donnelly. She was seated with her back to him, but her posture tensed as if she could feel him watching.

He quickly looked away, suddenly wishing he'd gone straight home tonight.

Since when are you a wuss? He ran into ex-girlfriends in Cielo Peak on a daily basis. Every encounter was different—with some women, he was on good enough terms for a friendly hug; with a few, he kept his distance. But the chance sightings never unsettled him.

Thankfully, the three men he was with resumed their harmless bickering. Justin joined in, harassing Washington about how long it had been since his last date. By the time their beer arrived, Justin's mood had improved.

Grainger kicked his foot under the table. "That leggy brunette at the end of the bar keeps eyeing you." He sounded wistful.

Justin grinned. "I'm sure you were her first choice until she spotted your wedding ring. From way over there."

The older man made a rude noise.

Justin didn't try to make his glance covert. Instead, he simply turned and found the woman in question—a brunette in an off-the-shoulder sweater and a pair of skinny jeans, spinning her barstool in slow half circles. He smiled at her, and she fluttered her fingers in an encouraging wave.

Chris Hyatt was craning his neck, trying to get a look. "Anyone you know?"

"Nope. Never seen her before," Justin said. "Which means she's probably visiting and the polite thing to do would be to ask how she's enjoying her stay. Or maybe she's moved here, in which case I should welcome our newest citizen." Either way, as a lifelong resident of Cielo Peak, it was practically his civic duty to go over there. Yet he remained where he was.

She's not a redhead.

It was an insane thought. He'd always admired

women of many different physical attributes, personalities and professions. He didn't have a "type." But his gaze strayed back to the corner where Elisabeth sat. The neon sign on the wall above her cast an otherworldly glow on her coppery hair. He toyed with the idea of taking the bull by the horns and marching to her table, just to prove to himself that he could. If it was true she'd gotten engaged, he could buy her table a bottle of whatever passed for champagne here.

He was mulling over the merits of this idea when Hyatt announced in an unsubtle stage whisper, "Incoming hottie."

The brunette? Justin swiveled in his seat, then sighed heavily. *Lina.* What had he done to deserve being accosted by her twice in one week? He stood, putting some distance between him and his buddies, potentially shameless eavesdroppers.

With her hair in loose curls over the shoulder of her knit dress, it was understandable that some men found her attractive. But all Justin felt when he looked at her was mild exasperation and confusion about why people called her the pretty Donnelly.

He kept his voice low. "Come to yell at me some more?"

She wasn't scowling tonight. Instead, she leaned into him, beaming as though he'd invented chocolate. "Do you know what I've realized? In the entire time we've known each other, I don't think you've ever asked me to dance." She put her hand on his arm and batted her lashes.

He was tempted to ask how many of the one-dollar

pitchers she'd enjoyed. But her gaze was alert and stony, belying the flirtatious tone of her voice.

"So how about it?" she purred. "Dance with me?"

As different as the Donnelly twins were, he knew they were as loyal to each other as he was to his own siblings. There was absolutely no way Lina would hit on her sister's ex-boyfriend, especially not right in front of Elisabeth. So what was going on?

Curiosity more than anything else prompted him to agree. "One dance."

The music was mostly masked by the cacophony of a packed bar, but buried beneath the ambient noise was a discernible bass line. He let her lead the way onto the floor, rolling his eyes when she tottered in a pair of high heels that were ridiculous for December. "You're going to sprain an ankle in those," he predicted.

"Nonsense. They're new. I'll be fine once they're broken in." She shimmied and wriggled to the beat. "Besides, they make my legs look fabulous." Pausing expectantly, she gave him a chance to agree, but he was unwilling to engage in the pseudo-flirting.

He retreated a step. "What are you up to?"

She sighed. "When I saw you at the ski shop, I'd just found out about Elisabeth's engagement and my emotions got the best of me."

"So you wanted to apologize?"

"Hell, no. Dancing with you serves a two-fold purpose. Elisabeth recently claimed she didn't give a rodent's butt who you date, and I'm challenging that assertion. Let's see if my dancing with you bothers her."

"It's bothering *me*," he muttered.

"Also, I never got around to what I actually meant to ask you on Sunday. I want you to talk to her."

"What?" He froze, abandoning even the halfhearted attempt at dancing. "Bad idea. She doesn't want advice from me."

"She doesn't want advice from anyone. I think she's trying to prove something about having control of her life and making savvy decisions but, Justin, I know my sister. She'll regret this. Steven gets here Thursday night—that's her fiancé."

The word scraped across his nerves like the sharp, unexpected sting of a paper cut.

"Promise me you'll talk to her before he arrives?" Lina cajoled. "It's a long shot, but maybe if you seem sorry you ended things—"

"I'm not. And I won't lie to her." Justin was not a great boyfriend. But he was, at the very least, honest with the women in his life.

"Then just ask her if she's happy. She's had years of practice managing me and our parents, and she keeps deflecting us. Maybe if you're the one who confronts her, you'll catch her off guard enough to make her think about it. Call her, and I'll never bother you again."

"I'm telling you, she won't listen to anything I say."

"Maybe, maybe not. How will you know if you don't try? I don't think you're prepared for how focused I am when I want something." She put her hands on her hips. "This is my hometown, too, Justin. We could run into each other a *lot* in the next few weeks."

He really, really should have gone straight home tonight. "Your parents are decent people. Do they know you're out threatening the populace?"

"Not the populace, slick, just you. Think I'm an un-stable pain in the ass now? Wait until the person who's always been the steadying influence in my life moves to California."

That far away? The information thudded to the pit of his stomach. "I'll call her before Thursday night." Even if Elisabeth hung up on him, he would have ful-filled his end of the bargain. "But the next time you spot me in a public place, Miss Donnelly? Forget you know me."

SINCE NONE OF the patrollers had seen their waitress in half an hour, Justin volunteered to go to the bar for a couple of waters and a coffee for Grainger. Trying to get through the crowd gave him some appreciation for what salmon had to endure to swim upstream. For the most part, all he could do was move when the crush of people around him did and try not to knock any-one over whenever movement halted—not that there was enough room for someone to actually fall in this throng.

The teeming mass thinned out slightly near the re-strooms as some reached their destination, but others entered the fray, trying to return to their tables. He found himself face-to-face, body to body, with Elisa-beth. Recognition burned through him, the visceral acknowledgment of this woman as his lover.

Ex-lover.

Very ex. But his five senses didn't register the change of status. Her dress reminded him of a trench coat, buttoned down the front and belted with a knot-ted sash. He wanted to tug it, to unwrap her. Unlike her sister's crazy five-inch heels, Elisabeth wore a pair of leather boots that disappeared beneath the hem of her dress. It suddenly seemed urgent to find out how high up those boots went.

Aware that her startled expression was blossoming into one of disapproval, he tried not to picture her wearing nothing but the boots.

Color climbed in her cheeks. "You're in my way."

"Or you're in mine," he countered with a grin. "Depends on how you look at it."

She huffed out a frustrated breath and angled her body sideways, wiggling so that she had room to pass between him and the wall to his left.

Follow the beautiful redhead or continue his trip to the bar? He changed direction before he even finished the thought. The bar could wait. "I don't know if you saw me on the dance floor with Lina—" who'd certainly been doing her part to sell the spectacle "—but nothing happened between us."

"That's why you're stalking me?" Elisabeth cast a quelling glance over her shoulder. "To clarify a meaningless dance with my mule-headed sister? Because I was *deeply* concerned about your publicly seducing her in the span of a three-minute song. Thank God you've cleared up the matter or I never would've been able to sleep tonight."

Her waspish sarcasm was invigorating. Everyone thought of Elisabeth Donnelly as levelheaded and reserved. It was a perverse point of pride that he could ruffle her feathers.

Now that they were farther from both the bar and the restrooms, there was more open space around them. He took advantage of the opportunity, gently steering her toward a recessed indentation in the wall. It was the kind of alcove that had probably housed a pay phone in the days before everyone carried a cell.

She swatted his hand away from her shoulder. "I have friends waiting for me." The light caught the diamond ring she wore.

"It's true, then." Seeing the proof of her engagement was different than hearing about it from Lina. Something unpleasant rippled through him, like the chills he'd experienced last time he had the flu. "You're getting married."

She met his gaze, her expression challenging. "Yes, I am."

"And moving away?"

"Not that it's any of your business, but yes. Heading to California, trading snowboards for surfboards." Her words had a rehearsed quality, as if she'd made the same crack to others. Her pinched expression didn't reveal any eagerness for the relocation.

"How's Kaylee feel about it?" he asked softly. Justin knew what it was like to lose a parent. He couldn't imagine how much worse it would have been for him as a kid if his aunt had uprooted him and his siblings, removing them from the warm support of the community.

Fury sparked in Elisabeth's eyes. "Don't you *dare* ask about her like some concerned friend or kindly uncle. You made it pretty clear you don't give a damn about either of us, or about anyone else but yourself."

The unexpected words wounded him. She couldn't really believe that, could she? "Now wait a—"

But she'd already twisted away and was merging back into the press of happily tipsy patrons. Justin's instincts screamed at him to follow, to plead his case, but the rational part of him knew it was smarter to let her go.

Letting her go had always been the right choice.

Chapter Three

Wednesday was a busy day on the mountain. Justin had reported for work at seven-thirty in the morning, starting with a rundown on the day's weather conditions and post assignments. Shortly after tourists began hitting the slopes, a skier had broken her wrist. Justin took her by toboggan to get medical attention. After an early lunch, he assisted with some training and taught a CPR class. The entire day felt like one fast-paced blur of activity, and before he knew it, he was in his SUV headed to Arden's for dinner.

His sister, like his ex-girlfriend, was also engaged to be married. Soon Arden would become Mrs. Garrett Frost. Garrett spent as much time in Cielo Peak as he could, but his family's ranch a couple of hours to the east required his attention. Whenever Garrett couldn't be in town, Justin made it a point to check in on Arden and two-month-old Hope. Plus, Arden was a terrific cook. It was no hardship to exchange the occasional night of his bachelor lifestyle for one of her home-cooked meals and the chance to cuddle his niece.

As much as Justin loved baby Hope, the day she'd been born had been one of the scariest of his life. Arden and Garrett had been temporarily estranged, and the cowboy hadn't been anywhere near Cielo Peak when Arden went into premature labor. Justin had been with her at the hospital while doctors explained the complications and dangers she faced. He'd been terrified he was about to lose another loved one.

When he was ten, his mom had died the week after Thanksgiving; his father passed away a few years later. Justin and Arden had been raised in part by an elderly aunt but mostly by their older brother, Colin. The Cade siblings had banded together in a tight family unit, which had expanded when Colin married. Tragedy lashed out at them again when a car accident took Colin's wife and toddler son. If anything had happened to Arden...

But she was fine, Justin reminded himself. His niece was a healthy, beautiful baby, and his sister was ecstatic about her February wedding. She made frequent jokes about how she and Garrett had approached their relationship backward, but Justin privately doubted she'd change a thing that had brought them to this point. She'd never been happier.

When he turned onto Arden's street, Justin's mouth fell open in disbelief. Her entire house was outlined in twinkling white lights. The trees in the yard were adorned with red and green bulbs that blinked in a frenetic pattern. A spotlight shone on an inflatable polar bear that seemed nearly as tall as Justin's six-foot-two height. A moving train circled the bear. Justin practically needed sunglasses to park in the driveway.

Since Arden was expecting him and he never knew when the baby might be asleep, he let himself in without knocking. "It's me," he called softly. He followed the mouthwatering smell of roast beef and the rhythmic sound of a mechanized baby swing to the kitchen.

Hope was safely harnessed into the reclining swing, watching the mobile of brightly colored animals above her head. Her eyelids were beginning to droop, though. She had the Cade eyes, the same deep blue-green that Justin and his siblings shared. Her hair was black like her father's, a much darker shade than Arden's or Justin's brown hair.

Justin dropped a quick kiss on his sister's forehead, then jerked his thumb toward the front of the house. "Don't you think your cowboy got a little carried away? It's like the freaking Vegas Strip out there."

"Isn't it great?" Arden beamed at him. "I admit, we probably went overboard, but…this is Hope's first Christmas. We want to make it special."

And *special* was synonymous with *able to see the house from space?* He bit back the reminder that Hope was only two months old and wouldn't even remember the seizure-inducing light show when she was older. Why allow his bah-humbug tendencies to ruin other people's joy?

Arden's smile faded, and her voice took on an audible ache. "Speaking of Christmas…our brother is dodging me."

"Left him a message a couple of weeks ago. He didn't return my call, either," Justin commiserated.

She banged a wooden spoon down next to the stove. "Thanksgiving was bad enough! Colin didn't come to town, and you took the holiday shift at the ambulance station."

"I didn't mind," he assured her. "I would've been in the way here. You and Garrett were still adjusting to the baby, and you needed the bonding time with your future in-laws."

She wasn't mollified. "No one's Thanksgiving should be limited to a couple of turkey slices on nutritionally bankrupt white bread! You only got away with it because in November, I was exhausted and recovering from the C-section. I was in no condition to pitch a fit. But I swear, if you and Colin aren't both here for Christmas, I will throw an unholy tantrum the likes of which you've never seen. It's more than Hope's first Christmas. It's my last one as a Cade. As much as I can't wait to marry Garrett, moving to the ranch will change things."

"It's not your last anything." He hugged her. "You'll always be a Cade."

"Will you try to talk to Colin? For me?"

Justin stifled a sigh. She was asking *him*—the guy who wanted to rip December off the calendar and skip straight into the New Year—to be her ambassador for a big family celebration? "All right. I'll get him here even if I have to track him down and toss him into the trunk of my SUV."

"Thank you." With that settled, she handed him a platter of roasted carrots and potatoes to carry to the table.

Throughout the meal, they chatted about their jobs. Arden, a professional photographer, regaled him with anecdotes of her afternoon trying to take a four-generation family portrait.

"There were twenty-eight of them! They wouldn't

fit in my studio, and it's too cold to shoot outside. We got to use the Cielo Peak performance hall because the family makes annual contributions and one of the sisters plays in the jazz ensemble. The great-grandfather nodded off twice while I was trying to arrange everyone. Between trying to keep him awake and trying to keep the toddler from fussing, it was the most challenging job I've had since the Cavanaugh wedding where the bride wanted a picture with her biological parents—a divorced couple who hadn't set foot in the same room in seventeen years."

That led into a discussion of Arden's own wedding plans, and Justin was happy to listen as he polished off the last of his roast beef. Or, at least, *half* listen. He would take a bullet for his sister, but he wasn't cut out for conversations about the color of pew-bows. So it took him by surprise when conversation halted, his sister peering at him as if awaiting a reply.

He stalled brilliantly. "Um..."

"You men can talk trivial sports statistics until the cows come home, but can't sit through five minutes of wedding updates! I asked if you thought you might bring a date to the ceremony. While it's customary to allow guests a plus-one, it's not like you're dating—"

"Untrue. I date all the time."

She rolled her eyes. "My point exactly. You don't have a girlfriend, and God knows Colin will come alone. Assuming he even attends."

The doubt in her tone was wrenching. "Hey, he wouldn't miss this for the world. He agreed to walk you down the aisle."

"I know. But...sometimes it feels like we've lost

him. I wonder if we should have tried harder to keep
him here instead of letting him roam the countryside,
doing odd jobs on ranches. This will sound stupid, but
I worry that if he drifts too far out of orbit, he won't be
able to find his way home."

Justin stood, clearing plates from the table. Would
it be cruel to point out that Colin had lost his wife and
child and probably needed distance from Arden, who
now had her own child and was about to become a
wife? No matter how sincerely Colin wanted his sister's happiness, her bliss couldn't be easy to be around.

After a moment, she joined him at the sink, her
earlier sadness replaced with an air of determination
that never boded well. She smiled. "Speaking of your
abysmal dating habits—"

"We weren't. We were discussing our drifter brother
and how we should save him from himself. Let's explore that further."

She ignored him. "Christmas is a special time."

It was eerie how much she sounded like their mother.
Arden had only been four when their mom got sick. Did
she remember that Christmas had been Rebecca Cade's
favorite time of year? Did Arden recall any of the traditions that had faded once their mom was gone? For
a second, the kitchen around him seemed filled with
the aroma of spicy sausage balls and the sharp sweet-
ness of lemon bars. He recalled the music of his mom's
laugh after she routinely tried—and failed—to hit the
high note in "O Holy Night."

"It's a time," Arden continued, "of reconnection.
Even if you haven't spoken to someone in months, you
can send them a card."

He narrowed his eyes. "Why do I think you mean 'someone' specific?"

"You never should have let her go." Arden's voice was soft, but the reproving note echoed all around him. "As I've said many times before, you and Elisabeth were great together."

"You have a point. Not about us being great, but about you saying it many, many times. Give it a rest, will you?"

"Colin has gone God knows where, so I can't help him. Maybe I still have a shot at getting you to fix your messes before I move to the ranch. I know we joke about your love life, but breaking up with Elisabeth Donnelly was the stupidest thing you've ever done."

It hadn't been stupidity. It had been self-preservation. But he couldn't explain to his happily engaged sister the claustrophobia he'd experienced during dinners with the Donnellys or the clawing panic as Elisabeth watched her friend Michelle succumb to the same disease that had taken his mother. His growing attachment to Elisabeth and her family had been uncomfortable enough, but then Kaylee had started visiting during some of her mom's hospital stays...

He cleared his throat, shoving the memories aside. "You don't have to worry about Elisabeth Donnelly. She's found some businessman. You can bet they have more in common than she and I ever did."

If Elisabeth decided to enter the corporate world, she was bright enough to fast-track herself to a fancy corner office and well-dressed minions. Meanwhile, Justin worked three different jobs in the course of a year to compensate for the off-season and lived in a rented house. His ambitions were about conquering black diamond trails, not making money or building a legacy.

"She has a boyfriend?" Arden frowned. "It's a small town, and I haven't seen her with anyone. Maybe it's not serious."

"Serious enough that he proposed and she said yes."

"What?"

He leaned against the counter, his pose relaxed. It was important that Arden saw how unbothered he was by Elisabeth's engagement. "They have a long-distance relationship—even longer distance than you and the cowboy. I ran into Lina on Sunday, and she filled me in on the details." He omitted the part about how Lina thought the engagement was a mistake and blamed Justin for her sister's rash decision.

"Oh." Arden's forehead furrowed into pensive lines. "I was so sure you and she…"

"Sis, I'm glad you found true love, but that doesn't give you magical insight into everyone else's personal lives." No matter how fervently she insisted he and Elisabeth belonged together, stubbornness did not equal truth. "No more unsolicited opinions, okay?"

She snorted. "Yeah, that's gonna happen."

As she brewed coffee to go with the chocolate-caramel brownies that were cooling, Arden brightened. "I always liked Elisabeth, but talking to her got weird after you broke up. Now that she's over you, I should call and compare notes on wedding gown shopping."

He made a noncommittal sound.

"And I have to keep reminding myself that Garrett fell into my life when I least expected it. Just because I was wrong about you and Elisabeth doesn't mean you're doomed to be alone." She poked him in the shoulder. "The right girl for you is out there."

God, I hope not. Because he'd rather ski blindfolded down the side of a mountain than meet her.

NINE O'CLOCK FOUND Justin sitting on his black leather couch, eyeing his cell phone as if it were a prairie rattlesnake. Earlier in the evening, he'd ignored a text from Lina asking if he'd made the promised call to her sister yet. She'd followed it up with another text reading, "You don't want to be on my bad side. I'm the evil twin."

He could dismiss Lina if she were his only motivating factor for contacting Elisabeth. But even though he'd told Arden that Elisabeth had happily moved on, he hadn't seen evidence of that happiness last night. If she were over Justin and in love with someone else, shouldn't she have been more philosophical about their breakup, less prickly? And, as hard as he'd tried, he couldn't shake the memory of Kaylee's wide brown eyes, far too solemn for a child that age. *Justin, is my momma gonna die?*

In his mind, he saw Kaylee's face but it was four-year-old Arden's voice he heard all over again. He hadn't been able to help Kaylee Truitt cope with the loss of her mother. Was there still a chance that he could do something useful for the kid? Elisabeth would resent the hell out of his questioning her decision, but since she seemed to hate him anyway, what did he have to lose?

Decision made, he picked up his phone and scrolled through the contact list. But he couldn't find Elisabeth or the Donnelly Ski Lodge, which puzzled him. He rarely bothered to update contact information and kept every number entered, including one for a take-out restaurant that had gone out of business two years ago and another simply marked *G*. Had he deleted Elisabeth?

The week after he'd left her—and simultaneously left his job—was hazy in recollection.

During the spring, Justin had worked at her family's lodge as a hiking guide. The Donnellys had been inescapable, woven into all corners of his life. Elisabeth's mother had made a huge fuss over his birthday. Mr. Donnelly, outnumbered by the women in his family, constantly expressed gratitude that he finally had an ally. It was disorienting. Fathers in Cielo Peak had always preferred Justin stay away from their daughters.

Had the Donnellys been quick to extend their approval to the new man in Elisabeth's life, or had they learned their lesson?

Justin reached for the phone book on the bottom ledge of his coffee table. As he dialed her number, he wondered if she'd even pick up when she saw who was calling.

Surprisingly, she did. "Hello?"

"Hey. It's Justin." *Now what?* He kicked his feet up onto the table, searching for the words that would make her agree to see him. The Cade charm was more effective in person—not that it had done much good last night. "Our conversation in the bar has been bothering me. If you're leaving Cielo Peak, that's not the way I want to end things between us."

"Justin, things between us ended long before last night."

Their relationship had ended when she told him she loved him and he'd told her goodbye. He'd wanted to apologize for the way it had happened dozens of times. But how could he when he knew that, under the same circumstances, he'd make the same decision again?

He stifled thoughts of the bittersweet past. "I should have offered my congratulations. How about I buy you lunch tomorrow?"

"To congratulate me on my engagement?" Her tone was heavy with skepticism.

"That, and to give us a chance to talk."

"What are we doing now?"

Hell if I know. But before he could come up with a better answer than "please meet me, or I'll need a restraining order against your sister," she inexplicably agreed.

"Actually," Elisabeth said, "I do have something I want to speak with you about."

"Really?" He couldn't imagine what. Despite Lina's crazy predictions, he doubted his opinions would carry any weight with Elisabeth. Not anymore.

"If you don't mind an early lunch," she said, "I can make a little time in my schedule. Eleven-thirty? At the lodge?"

"Your family's lodge?" He'd managed to avoid setting foot inside since they'd stopped dating.

"Is that a problem?"

"No." But it gave her a whopping home-field advantage. "Meet you at the front desk." The words rolled off his tongue from force of habit. How many times had he said that exact phrase during the months when they'd worked together? Some of his most unforgettable romantic encounters had started with her smiling from the other side of that reception desk. An avalanche of memories threatened to bury him.

"R-right, front desk." For the first time since answering her phone, she sounded hesitant. "See you then."

IT WAS DIFFICULT for Justin to fall asleep Wednesday night—his head was too full of female voices. Lina's, dripping accusation; Arden's, predicting that love was lying in wait for him around some dark corner; Elisabeth's, vibrating with the hint of unshed tears when he'd told her they should stop seeing each other. And in the background of his cluttered thoughts, his mom's voice lingered, singing off-key Christmas carols.

After a restless night of fragmented dreams, he gave up and climbed out of bed Thursday morning an hour before his alarm clock would have blared. With the extra time, maybe he could stop at the Cielo Café bakery counter, pick up a few dozen bagels and muffins for the patrol team. But once he got behind the wheel of his SUV, he found himself driving in the wrong direction. Ten minutes later, he parked at the cemetery, not quite sure what he was doing there.

It had been a long time since he'd visited. Colin refused to come here, and Arden had been so busy with the pregnancy and the new baby.

Jamming his gloved hands in the pockets of his coat, Justin crunched across the layer of snow frosting the walkway. There was a stark beauty in how the rising sun illuminated the headstones. Parts of the cemetery were still in shadow, but other patches, beginning to catch the dawn, shone brilliantly. He tried to appreciate the sight rather than think about how row after row symbolized people who had once been loved and were now gone.

A grandfather he'd never known had purchased family plots here, but Justin had no intention of being buried. He'd told Arden that when the time came, he wanted to be cremated, his ashes scattered on the wind. She'd made morbid jokes. "So even after you die, you refuse to settle down? Sounds about right."

As he reached his parents' joint marker, he suddenly felt sheepish, as if he'd tracked mud into his mother's clean kitchen. "I should have brought flowers." Something seasonal, like poinsettias. "I know you loved Christmas, Mom, but it hasn't been the same since you died."

That first year, his father had been too devastated to remember the holiday. If it weren't for the gentle interference of their aunts, the Cade children wouldn't have had anything to unwrap Christmas morning. Then they lost their dad, too. Throughout Justin's adolescence, they'd occasionally accepted invitations to join well-meaning families in the community, but it was awkward, being the gloomy thundercloud that hung over someone else's festivities. They got in the habit of staying home, where Colin microwaved dinner and the two brothers taught Arden how to play cards. That's what the holiday season had become for Justin—rubbery lasagna and explaining blackjack to his sister.

Now, he survived November to January by hoping for good ski conditions and ignoring the hectic whirl of shopping, decorating and televised specials.

His mind slipped to the Donnellys. While he'd never been inside their house around Christmas, he imagined it was thoroughly decorated. After all, Mrs. Donnelly had gone to great efforts simply for his birthday— streamers and humorous miniposters, balloons on the mailbox and an elaborate home-cooked meal. They were a close-knit family who liked to celebrate together.

Yet Elisabeth was choosing to move away. Brushing his hand over the smooth, cold edge of his parents' gravestone, he couldn't help but wonder, did she have any idea what she was giving up?

Chapter Four

Elisabeth finished drying her hands and consulted her watch. 11:28 a.m. She should hurry back out to the lobby and—

No. No hurrying. She wasn't some sixteen-year-old eager to see her boyfriend. She was a grown woman who was doing Justin a favor by meeting him. Frankly, her schedule was already full. The lodge was doing brisk holiday business, and Steven was arriving tonight. She'd shuffled several tasks to squeeze in this lunch. It might do Justin some good to wait a few minutes.

Taking her time, she pulled her brush and lipstick out of her purse, but then stopped. She might not want to rush on Justin Cade's behalf, but she wasn't about to primp for him, either. *He* was not the reason she'd dressed that morning in formfitting black jeans and a gold sweater that was both festive and complemented her coloring. No, if she'd put any extra care into her appearance, it was for her fiancé.

She pushed open the door to the ladies' room and made her way through the evergreen-scented lobby. In addition to the fourteen-foot tree the staff had helped decorate, Elisabeth and her father had hung a dozen wreaths throughout the main building. Currently, her dad was working a shift as ski lift operator, and she hoped he'd stay out of the main building while Justin was here. For a month after the breakup, Graham Donnelly had threatened daily to "give that bounder a piece of my mind."

Elisabeth had also gently maneuvered her mother, Patti, into leaving the premises. The school system's two-week winter break kicked off today with an early release for students. Patti was picking up Kaylee from school and taking her to lunch. As difficult as the past few months had been for Kaylee, the one bright spot had been watching a girl who'd never had an extended family blossom under the attention of doting grandparents and a conspiratorial aunt.

Thoughts of Kaylee's lunch plans scattered when Elisabeth locked eyes with her own lunch date. Justin leaned against the corner of the reception desk. Though his body language was relaxed, he had that intense, hyperalert gaze that had so often caused her stomach to flutter. Of all her reasons to be angry with him, that gaze topped the list.

Elisabeth wasn't naive—she'd heard rumors about Justin before dating him. But since she didn't let gossip make her decisions for her, she'd gone out with him, prepared to make up her own mind. In spite of his flirtatious, skirt-chasing reputation, he'd never looked at another female when he was with Elisabeth. He'd smiled absently when a cute waitress fawned over him without ever taking his eyes off his date.

When he'd unceremoniously dumped her, he'd reminded her, "I told you I wasn't looking for anything serious. I didn't lie." But he had. Not verbally, but with his actions. He'd made her feel adored and singularly special.

While she and Kaylee were in New Mexico visiting Steven, he'd apologized for being preoccupied with the software update his company was about to release. Frankly, Elisabeth found it a relief to be with someone who didn't constantly make her feel like the center of his universe. The heady euphoria wasn't worth the harsh disillusionment.

She didn't realize how reluctant her steps had become until Justin gave up waiting on her and met her halfway, moving with that unconscious swagger of his. Damn it. Even the way the man walked was irritating.

He took her hand between both of his. "Beth. You look great." There was a raspy quality to his deep voice that always made his words sound more intimate than they should.

"Elisabeth," she corrected, withdrawing her hand. "No one calls me Beth." She wasn't the type of person who inspired nicknames. As a child, she'd been shy and serious—the worrier on the sidelines who did her best to keep her reckless twin out of trouble. As an adult, Elisabeth only revealed her fun-loving side to a select few. She commanded a sizable staff and sometimes had to deal with difficult guests. People needed to take her seriously.

She ignored the undignified memory of shrieking with laughter as Justin tickled her one morning. Justin didn't do "serious." At least, not in his personal life.

"I asked the restaurant manager to have a table

ready." She was proud of her casual tone. No reason to get emotional about this. "I can spare about half an hour."

He nodded. "Same here. Lead the way."

In the evenings, a hostess seated diners, but during the slower day shifts while many guests were on the slopes, restaurant manager Javier Ortiz did double duty. Javier, a slim man with salt-and-pepper hair, had started as a busboy when Elisabeth was in sixth grade. When he saw her with Justin, he did an almost comical double take.

"Señor Cade. It has been a long time." He cut his dark eyes toward Elisabeth, as if seeking guidance on whether he should be happy to see Justin. Whatever Javier glimpsed in her posture or face led him to instruct, "This way, Señor" in a clipped tone he never would have used with a guest.

After they were seated, Justin shook his head with a self-deprecating smile. "I think it's safe to say I'm no longer on Javier's Christmas card list." He tapped his napkin-wrapped silverware. "In fact, I kind of got the feeling he might come at me with one of these knives."

She unrolled her own cloth napkin and studied the butter knife. "If it makes you feel better, I doubt these would do much damage." She paused a beat. "But I suppose he could always grab one from the kitchen."

"He wouldn't be the first to ambush me this week. Do you know your sister recently threatened to tear me limb from limb?"

"Lina?" It was a dumb response—she had only one sister. *One highly confusing and increasingly erratic sister.* When Elisabeth had announced her engagement,

Lina seemed to take the news as a personal affront. Next she'd overcompensated by acting as if they were teenage BFFs who should be together or be texting every waking second. Finally, and most bizarrely, Lina had thrown herself at Justin on the dance floor with all the subtlety of a brick.

Then again, a case could be made for throwing bricks at Justin.

While Elisabeth momentarily indulged in that fantasy, he'd begun speaking again. "Lina and I saw each other at the sporting goods shop. She was pretty angry, ranting at me that your engagement is…might be emotional fallout from… There's no way to say this without sounding like a deluded egomaniac."

"You've never let that stop you before," she said sweetly.

"Does your moving away have anything to do with me?"

The question shocked her into silence. Is that what he thought? Justin and Lina considered Elisabeth so pathetic she'd let an ex-boyfriend run her out of town?

She kept her voice calm and low. One might even say detached. "You stopped having influence on my life the day you broke up with me." Well, later that same week, anyway. There may have been a weepy, seventy-two hour period of hoping he'd come to his senses that she didn't like to recall.

"Good." He gave her a relieved smile. "Glad to hear it. Please be sure to tell your sister."

"Oh, trust me, she'll be getting an earful." Elisabeth would already be headed up to the third floor for a sisterly chat if Lina weren't with a client right now. It had been Lina's idea to offer some limited day-spa services, which helped them generate income even after the snows melted for the year. Her hot stone massages were proving to be a big hit.

Instead of a waitress, Javier himself came to the table for their orders. "Your usual salad, Señorita Donnelly?" He waited for her nod, then glowered at Justin. "And what do *you* want?"

It was an excellent question, in Elisabeth's opinion. What on earth did Justin want? Even if Lina's crazy suspicion had been true and Elisabeth was rebounding, why would he care? He'd walked away from Elisabeth—and by extension, Kaylee—without a backward glance. Was he feeling some sort of belated guilt? Maybe it was one of those Dickensian situations, where he'd been visited by three ghosts who'd made it clear what a cad he was.

None of that was her problem. She had Steven and a bright, sensible future awaiting her.

Once Javier had gone, Justin leaned forward, his eyes earnest. "Obviously, Lina has some of her wires crossed, but just because she was wrong about your reasons for going to California doesn't mean she's wrong about everything. She's afraid you might regret this move, and she could be right. You've never been so far from your family."

After this week, she wasn't sure California was far *enough* from her meddling sister. *Maybe I should ask Steven more about his company's European offices.*

"And you've got Kaylee to consider," he added.

Despite her constant self-reassurance that she would not let Justin get to her, her temper flared. "You think

I don't know that? You think that's not on my mind when I fall asleep at night and still there when I wake up in the morning? Raising a daughter is a massive responsibility. She needs structure in her life and as much security as I can possibly give her, which is why I'm lucky to have met a man like Steven Miller."

"I wasn't implying that you take your responsibilities lightly." Justin held up his hands in a placating gesture. "But, since you've never actually been away from your family, you might not understand how hard it will be. On both of you. Wait, his last name is Miller? Like The Steve Miller Band?"

Before she could respond, a child's excited squeal interrupted. "Justin!"

Elisabeth whipped her head around, dismay pooling inside her. *Oh, no. She's not supposed to be here.* Kaylee, showing more enthusiasm than she'd exhibited for anything since the monkeys at the Albuquerque Zoo, was hurtling toward them, joy lighting her small face.

Trailing behind was Elisabeth's mother. At fifty-four, Patti Donnelly's red hair was faded and her figure was slightly plumper than in her younger years, but she was as lively as when she'd taught her girls how to hokeypokey on roller skates two decades ago. Her round, cherubic face, which usually made her look younger than her age, was crinkled in agitation. Although she didn't question Elisabeth outright on Justin's presence, her raised eyebrows spoke volumes.

"I haven't seen you in forever and ever," Kaylee declared, scrambling into Justin's lap.

When the little girl had first met him, he'd earned her eternal affection with humorous impressions of every major character on SpongeBob SquarePants. Kaylee still asked when he'd come visit her but, mercifully, those requests had become less frequent. The last thing Elisabeth wanted was for the child to get attached to him all over again. She needed to explain that this lunch was for adult conversation.

"Kaylee—"

"Elisabeth, dear, might I have a word with you?" her mom interjected. "Lodge business. Should only take a moment."

Lodge business, huh? Elisabeth suspected that was code for maternal interrogation. Nonetheless she followed her mother to an unoccupied corner of the dining room. "I thought you and Kaylee were having lunch in town," she said pointedly.

"I told her she could pick any place she wanted, but you know how much she adores Chef Bates."

Elisabeth would never forget the first night she and Kaylee had arrived home after the funeral in Denver. Worrying that Kaylee had barely eaten in days, Elisabeth had been anxious to get some food into her. But the kid-friendly suggestions she'd offered—everything from grilled cheese to chocolate cake—had reminded Kaylee of things her mother used to cook. The girl had dissolved into body-wracking sobs. In a fit of desperation, Elisabeth had pulled out a container of leftover black ink risotto that she'd brought home from a fancy event at the lodge.

Kaylee had been intrigued enough to try a bite. Even though she hadn't immediately loved it, she wanted to know what else Elisabeth had in her fridge that came from Chef Bates. The six-year-old plowed through some lobster ravioli, then fell into an exhausted sleep on Elisabeth's sofa. After that, finding exotic foods for her to try had become a coping mechanism for them. There would be no chicken nuggets like her mom used to serve for lunch or chocolate chip pancakes that Michelle cooked on her birthday. Luckily, lots of meals were exotic to a young child who'd never been outside of Colorado.

Patti's hazel eyes narrowed. "Maybe I would have done a better job of keeping her away from Justin if I'd *known* he was going to be on the premises. Why on earth is he here?"

Because your other daughter is a lunatic. "We just had a few things to discuss. You know his sister, Arden, is a photographer? I'd like to do an engagement photo with Steven while he's here this weekend. We might even hire her for the wedding."

"You want your ex-boyfriend's sister to take your wedding pictures?"

"Possibly. But I figured the courteous approach was to ask him first. So you see, our having lunch together isn't noteworthy. I would have preferred keeping Kaylee away, though. Once the shock of losing Michelle started to wear off, she was crushed to realize Justin wouldn't be part of our lives. I don't want her to suffer that disappointment again."

Patti reached out and smoothed a strand of Elisabeth's hair. "I know exactly how you feel. I've…never seen you so lost over a boy as you were when he walked away."

Boy? Elisabeth stole a glance back at their table.

Justin Cade—thirty years old, sexy as sin and the best skier she'd ever met in her life—was no boy.

"I don't want him to hurt you again," Patti insisted. "Are you sure you're all right with his being here? Say the word, and I'll have Javier throw him out on his ass."

Elisabeth covered her mouth with her hand to smother a giggle. "That won't be necessary, Mom. All I need you to do is pry Kaylee away from him. Don't worry, Justin can't hurt me."

Dating him had been like a cruel vaccine. He'd done so much damage the first time around that now she was immune.

JUSTIN HAD ALWAYS been fond of Kaylee Truitt. Yet he couldn't help wishing that Elisabeth and her mother would finish their discussion and rescue him. The pixie-faced girl with her corkscrew curls and glittery purple sweatshirt looked harmless, but she had an uncanny knack for mixing the trivial and the tragic, always finding the cracks in his armor.

She'd gone from telling him why the orange crayon at school was better than the blue one to demanding to know why he hadn't come over to play since she'd moved to Cielo Peak. Feeling like slime, he'd stammered something about being busy and recently becoming an uncle, relieved when she moved on to asking if he'd ever eaten squid and if he knew the difference between squid and octopus.

Then she looked him square in the eye and asked, "Do you think Santa can do anything to bring my mom back?"

His lungs burned with the sudden difficulty of

breathing, and his arms squeezed around her in a quick, reflexive hug. "No. I'm sorry, kiddo, but not even the big guy from the North Pole can help you with this one." He was jolted through time to that first December without *his* mom. That year, he'd been ashamed of every toy he'd ever asked for—none of them mattered. He would've given up toys and video games and candy for the rest of his life to have her back.

"I'm sorry about your mother." He touched his forehead to Kaylee's. "Mine's gone, too, and I miss her. But your mom knew that Beth—Elisabeth—is going to take really good care of you. And that Elisabeth loves you. Just remember you're not alone, okay?"

The damp sparkle in her eyes was like a punch in the stomach. *Don't cry, kid.* He didn't think he could take it.

He began babbling, trying to stave off her tears. "It's not just Elisabeth who loves you but her whole family. Her parents, the employees here at the lodge, your crazy aunt Lina. And I hear your family's going to get bigger soon, when Elisabeth gets married. I bet you'll have a really pretty dress to wear to the ceremony."

Kaylee wrinkled her nose. "She's marrying *Steven*. He doesn't like me."

"What? That can't be true." He pulled back to study her expression and gauge her sincerity.

"We stayed at his house, but he didn't want to play with me. He worked on his computer the whole time. He wouldn't even stop to watch SpongeBob."

"Maybe he likes you just fine, but he doesn't like SpongeBob." What the heck was taking Elisabeth so long? He wasn't qualified as a family counselor. "Try other cartoons. Give him some, er, Bugs Bunny DVDs for Christmas." Did kids still know who Bugs Bunny was?

"Christmas presents go under the tree. We don't have a tree." Her tone vibrated with anxiety, and her lower lip trembled. "Does that mean I don't get any presents?"

"Hey, no worries. You'll have presents," he assured her. "There's *plenty* of time to get a tree. I haven't picked mine out, either." No point in telling her that he never bothered with one.

"Picked what out?" Elisabeth asked suspiciously as if he might be plotting with a six-year-old behind her back. He was so relieved by her return that he wasn't even offended.

"Christmas trees," Kaylee answered. "Can we get one today? Justin can go with us!"

"Actually, kiddo, I have to get back to work." He tried to sound chagrined instead of eager to be rid of her. "Trails to groom, conditions to check, people to save."

A waitress arrived with plates of food, and Kaylee groaned that she was *staaarving*. Did that mean the little girl and Elisabeth's mother would be joining them? If so, the already strained level of awkwardness for this lunch date was about to rocket to mythic proportions.

Patti, who seemed even less happy to see him than the hostile restaurant manager, held out a hand to her granddaughter. "How about we visit Chef Bates and see what he can whip up for you?"

That brightened Kaylee's expression. She lowered herself from Justin's lap but paused to pin Elisabeth with an impatient glare. "When are we gonna get a tree?"

"How about tomorrow? I have to work until at least three, but we could go after that. And since Steven gets here tonight, he can come with us. Won't that be nice?"

Kaylee grimaced.

"Let's get you some food," Patti intervened. "Being hungry makes us cranky."

Justin watched them go, then turned back to Elisabeth. "She doesn't seem too enthusiastic about a new stepfather."

Emotion flared in her clear green eyes. She looked as if she wanted to argue or tell him to mind his own business, but her composure won out. "It will be an adjustment," she admitted calmly. "We'll get through it together. That's what families do."

Her statement struck a chord with him. How would he and Arden and Colin have coped without each other? And how would Justin manage when both his siblings were gone? An unfamiliar sensation speared him, and it took a moment to identify the pang as loneliness. *Ridiculous.* Between buddies and beautiful women, Justin was never alone.

He poked at his food. "You mentioned last night that you had something to discuss?"

She nodded. "With Steven in town this weekend, we have a small window of opportunity for engagement pictures. And I was wondering…would it be weird for you if I hired Arden? I was thinking she might be a good candidate for the wedding if she's not already booked that weekend."

"She's a great candidate," he said loyally. "Her work is terrific."

"So it won't bother you at all?" she prodded.

"Why should it?"

Her lips compressed into a thin line. "Right. Silly of me to think it might." She set down her fork. "I know I said you could have thirty minutes, but Mom alerted me to a guest problem that needs to be addressed. Since we've concluded our business here…"

"Don't let me keep you." He stood, reaching for his wallet. "I should get going, too." His obligation to Lina was fulfilled. He'd given Elisabeth his unsolicited opinion on raising a child, and now he wanted to get out of here before the tension between them got any worse. Or Kaylee had a chance to ask him any more difficult questions like why he wasn't her friend anymore.

Elisabeth shook her head when he pulled cash out of his billfold. "You don't have to pay for this."

Oh, but he already was. He followed her back to the lobby, trying not to notice the flattering way her jeans hugged her butt. In the past five months, he'd almost forgotten how fascinated he'd been with her composed nature, how he delighted in the challenge of getting her to open up to him. She was so cool and calm that every time she revealed an emotion—whether anger or laughter or something more vulnerable—had been like a victory. It had become addictive, helping her cultivate her responsive side and knowing he was one of the lucky few to glimpse it.

But encouraging her to be free with her feelings had come back to bite him on the ass when she'd fallen for him harder than he'd ever anticipated. Hadn't he warned her that he had no long-run potential? How could a woman with her intelligence want something lasting with *him?* He was the guy who'd practically broken out in hives whenever Patti Donnelly hugged him or Graham Donnelly had called him "son." *Well, you certainly solved that dilemma.* Now the Donnellys wanted nothing to do with him.

From around the corner, there came the pounding slap of footsteps, and a defeated-sounding woman issued a listless reminder not to run. Then two tall boys, not quite teenagers, zoomed into view. At their current speed, they were in danger of mowing over Elisabeth. Justin instinctively pulled her out of the collision course and against him.

The instant her body touched his, his mind went blank, heat silencing his intended reprimand to the hooligans. Elisabeth's sharp intake of breath was audible and, from his view over her shoulder, did mesmerizing things for her cleavage.

She craned her head to look up at him. "Thanks." The word ended on a near whisper as their gazes locked. She was right there, so close, in his arms the way she'd been hundreds of times before. The urge to kiss her was so natural....

"Justin?" Her voice was a squeak of uncertainty, jarring him from lust-addled memories.

He immediately dropped his hands to his sides, hoping he looked more innocent than he felt. "Just wanted to make sure you didn't get hurt."

A hollow chuckle escaped her. "Ironic, coming from you."

He flinched. "Guess I deserved that."

What about what *she* deserved? If she'd found a man worthy of her—if Lina's reservations were misplaced—then Justin had no right jeopardizing her future. He took a step back, trying to repress the desire he'd felt, trying to repress memories of how exquisitely responsive she'd always been to his kisses.

"I should go," she stammered. "I have a lot to wrap up before Steven gets into town."

"You kids have fun this weekend."

"Right." Her smile was tinged with sadness. "Fun."

He knew without her saying it that she was looking for something more profound than fun. Just as he knew it was all he'd ever be able to offer a woman.

WHEN LINA APPEARED in the doorway of the lodge's main office Thursday afternoon, Elisabeth shot to her feet. Her wheeled chair flew backward across the hardwood. "I don't know what kind of incense you burn during those relaxation therapy sessions, but I'm giving you the benefit of the doubt that you were high on some crazy New Age fumes when you decided to talk to Justin Cade about my engagement."

Lina froze, glancing over her shoulder as if debating whether it was too late to retreat.

"I'll chase you down," Elisabeth threatened. "You can't possibly outrun me in those heels."

Sighing, Lina entered the room where Elisabeth and Graham Donnelly worked. With two desks facing each other, the office was cramped yet cozy. Although Patti Donnelly chipped in with reservations and overseeing the housekeeping staff, she didn't hold a full-time position at the lodge. Lina's smaller workspace was on the third floor. She focused on new products for facials and making visitors feel welcome—she'd said more than once that if they put her in charge of accounting or inventory, the place would be out of business in a month.

Looking as guilty as a kid in the principal's office, Lina slid into their dad's chair. "Okay, I get why you're peeved."

"*Peeved?* I'm debating throwing this stapler at your head."

"No, you aren't." Lina laughed. "You'd never do anything like that. Although I must say, this is feistier than I've seen you in a long time. Don't you think that means something, your tapping into this much emotion on the same day you had lunch with Justin? Mom told me about it."

Elisabeth repositioned her chair and sat. "The emotion I'm demonstrating is toward *you,* my Benedict Arnold of a sister, not some ex." Some ex who'd almost kissed her in plain view of employees and guests.

A shiver ran down her spine. Had Justin been about to kiss her, or had she imagined it? Worse, had she really considered, for one brief self-destructive moment, letting him? *No, of course not.* But the refusal was unconvincing. Shame boiled through her. All right she had considered it—for a millisecond. Maybe it was as simple as misguided sense memory, her body's conditioned reaction to being in those strong arms, breathing in his familiar scent.

"You okay, sis? You look…flustered," Lina said.

"I am! Put yourself in my shoes. Christmas is just around the corner, I have a wedding to plan, Mom and Dad are formally meeting my fiancé tonight, I recently became a mother—and to top it all off, you randomly decided that I needed to deal with an ex-boyfriend?"

Lina ducked her head, her expression appropriately sheepish. "That may have been a bad call on my part. But whenever Mom or I ask if you're sure you're doing the right thing, you get dismissive. Strategy called for a different approach. Ergo, Justin."

Reminding herself that her sister meant well, Elisabeth tried not to grind her teeth. "You've confused dismissive with confident. And your track record with giving advice… Remember when we were nineteen, you convinced me my hair would look good highlighted, and it ended up bright orange? Or when I was hesitant about sleeping with a lodge employee, and you convinced me to go for it? *Not* that I blame you for what happened with Justin," she stressed. "I'm only saying that sometimes an observer thinks her opinion is right but doesn't have all the inside information. Besides, how come you get to interfere but never have to take my advice?"

Lina rolled her eyes. "If I took your advice, I'd be dating that really boring loan officer who works at the bank."

"As opposed to the guitarist who broke dates with you whenever he had a last-minute opportunity for a gig."

"He was a mistake. But I admitted he was a mistake. I didn't agree to marry him."

"Steven is not a mistake. You'll see that tonight, when we all have dinner." Elisabeth had first met Steven Miller when he'd come to Cielo Peak for a corporate retreat. His group had done some skiing interspersed with team building exercises and downtime. Her parents had probably seen him around the lodge, but when Elisabeth gave him permission to contact her once he returned to Albuquerque, she'd had no idea their relationship would become so serious.

"I guess it wasn't fair for me to judge him without meeting him, but—"

"No! There is no 'but.' There is only my twin sister being supportive. Do not make me kill you and hide the body in the Cupboard of Doom." She jerked her thumb over her shoulder, and Lina snorted in response at the running family joke.

The wall behind Elisabeth was covered in decorative panels, one of which was actually the door to a heavily cluttered storage area. The Donnellys joked about Hoffa's missing body being in the cabinet somewhere. During her late teens, Elisabeth had gradually taken on more and more responsibility at the lodge, getting her father organized in the process. But the storage space represented the many years prior to her intervention—a veritable cave of misfiled paperwork, boxes of memorabilia, obsolete personnel records and ugly artwork that had once hung upstairs. Graham Donnelly hadn't wanted to throw out the artwork since they were part of the lodge's "rich history."

Every once in a while, Elisabeth or her mother would remark that someone really should clean out the Cupboard of Doom. But they were all afraid of the avalanche they'd trigger by opening the door. For the most part, they pretended the cabinet didn't exist, although Lina had once suggested that, for liability reasons, they should cross over the door with pieces of yellow *Caution* tape.

"You couldn't fit my body in there. With as much junk as Daddy has crammed in, I doubt we could fit a paper clip." Lina's teasing smile faded. "Who's going to keep him organized once you're gone?" By which she undoubtedly meant, who was going to run this place when he decided it was time to retire? Elisabeth had long been the heir apparent.

"I don't know. But the chance to finally clean out the Cupboard of Doom isn't enough of a reason to stay," Elisabeth said. "Kaylee was so grief-stricken when I brought her to live with me. I know she'll miss Michelle no matter where we live, but we can make new associations in California." And they could leave behind the parts of their past best forgotten.

Chapter Five

"Thank you so much for having me in your home. Dinner was delicious." From his seat next to Elisabeth, Steven raised his wineglass in an appreciative toast to Patti Donnelly.

She smiled back at him. "Glad you enjoyed your meal." She'd been her usual amiable self tonight. Without time to privately ask her mother's thoughts, Elisabeth couldn't tell how much her mom liked him as a prospective son-in-law, but she clearly didn't *dis*like him. It was a start.

Her dad had been more standoffish. He was the one they'd need to win over because he was the one who'd been the most upset about his oldest daughter leaving the lodge. Elisabeth bit her bottom lip. In California, she could explore other job options. Or be a stay-at-home mom for Kaylee. After so many years of everyone assuming she'd run the lodge after her father, having choices should feel liberating. *It will be fine,* she told herself. Change built character.

Elisabeth tried to draw her dad into conversation. "Steven has never been snowmobiling. Weren't you planning a ride with some friends this weekend?"

Her fiancé leaned back in his chair. "I wouldn't want to impose. I—"

"Nonsense." Patti jabbed her husband with her elbow. "Graham would love for you to join them. Wouldn't you, honey?"

Elisabeth seized the opportunity to carry some plates into the adjacent kitchen in the hopes that the two men into her life, having been prompted, would fall into more natural conversation. She wasn't surprised when Lina joined her less than a minute later. Elisabeth knew her twin had probably been itching for a chance to share her opinion.

"Well?" Elisabeth kept her voice soft enough that no one would hear her over the running water as she rinsed dishes in the sink.

"He's cute," Lina said. "I didn't expect that."

Steven had gray eyes, classical features and thick blond hair. He wasn't especially tall, but neither was Elisabeth.

"You thought he'd be unattractive?"

"Not exactly. You just sound so…platonic when you talk about him. Sort of an implied 'he has a good personality.' But it's like you said earlier today, I'm an outsider and don't have all the facts. Maybe I was wrong, and there is heat between you."

Elisabeth said nothing. Heat wasn't her priority. She wanted a partner, not a radiator.

Lina jabbed her lightly in the side, a habit she'd clearly inherited from their mother. "Is he, you know, *good?*"

"Are you really asking me about sex with our parents only a few yards away?"

"That isn't a reassuring answer. Don't you—"

"We're waiting, not that it's any of your business. So you'll just have to wait until after the wedding for the full report." That last bit was sarcastic. She had zero intention of giving her sister a play-by-play.

"Waiting?" Lina's shocked voice was appallingly loud.

"Shhh! I don't know why you're so stunned. We're not the first couple in the history of the world to wait for the wedding night—and it isn't as if we have much longer to wait. Most of our relationship has been long-distance anyway, and the last thing we want to do is set a bad example for Kaylee."

"I see." Lina arched an eyebrow. "And those times you kept Kaylee at your place while you were dating Justin? You and he never...?"

Elisabeth's face heated as she recalled a frenzied and unexpectedly intense late-night encounter in her laundry room.

"Uh-huh. That's what I thought," her sister said smugly.

"Completely different situations. For one thing, he and I had already established a physical relationship. And Kaylee wasn't having nightmares then." Those began after Michelle's death. Elisabeth couldn't think of a less sexy first time than to have her and Steven's lovemaking interrupted by a sobbing child. *All three of us would need therapy.* "Steven's offered to sleep on my couch while he's in town. He's a real gentleman."

Lina gave her a smile so dubious it bordered on pitying.

"Stop looking like you feel sorry for me." Elisabeth

held up her left hand and waggled her fingers. "I'm the one with the good-looking fiancé and the diamond on her hand, remember? Living the dream."

"Funny." Lina squinted at her, the mischief fading from her gaze. "I was always the one with the dreams of becoming the princess of a tropical island or running off to join a rock band. I thought your dream was to take over the lodge eventually and raise kids of your own in Cielo Peak."

"Yeah, well." Elisabeth glanced toward the dining room. "Dreams change."

OCCASIONALLY, AFTER JUSTIN helped save someone, he received a thoughtful thank-you note or baked goods. On Friday afternoon, he helped save a freaked out twelve-year-old girl and received some minor bruises and lacerations. He discovered that trying to handle a panicking adolescent was a bit like trying to bathe a cat. Since he ended up with a gash courtesy of the girl's ski, his supervisor sent him into town for a tetanus shot and told him they'd see him tomorrow.

After swinging by the doctor's office, Justin intended to go home. He didn't have any ulterior motives. But when he spotted the sign for the locally owned Christmas tree farm...

He glanced at the digital clock in his dashboard. It was four o'clock. Had Elisabeth made good on her promise to take Kaylee tree-shopping? There was another place out by the highway they could have gone, but that lot hosted a temporary vendor who would be gone by December twenty-sixth and had no real ties to town. If he knew Elisabeth, she'd want to support the community.

As if his SUV had a will of its own, the vehicle made an unscheduled turn. A moment later, he found himself on a bumpy road leading to the customer parking lot. Sure enough, there was Elisabeth's car. She must be here somewhere, with Steven. Was the man worthy of her? He heard Kaylee's voice in his head. *He doesn't like me.* Having grown up with a younger sister—and dealing with a shrieking girl this afternoon—Justin knew that there were some instances of melodrama. Was Kaylee's aversion to the man a knee-jerk reaction to the news that she was leaving? Or was there any real basis for her complaint?

He stepped out of the SUV into the bracing cold. Nearby was a large striped tent with electric cords running beneath the canvas, most likely for space heaters. He supposed he should start there and get information on how selecting and purchasing a tree worked. Until now, he hadn't considered buying one, but why not? He was here; he might as well support the local economy, too. Nothing that would eat up too much space in the house he rented, just a simple, modestly sized tree.

As he entered the tent, he immediately spotted a dozen people he knew. Including Elisabeth. She stood out like a beacon in a bright blue coat. Kaylee was similarly eye-catching in lime-green and a headband with felt reindeer antlers. With them was a short man with hair the color of wheat. Steven?

Only one way to find out. He strode in their direction.

Elisabeth's eyes widened when she saw him, and

she hurried to meet him. It might have been flattering if she didn't give the impression that she was trying to run him off. "What are you doing here?" she hissed. "Stalking me?"

Pretty much. "Of course not. I'm here to get a tree, like everyone else."

"Justin!" Kaylee launched herself at him in what was probably intended as a hug but was executed as a tackle worthy of the Denver Broncos. He knelt down to return the embrace. "We got a tree, a real big one. Are you gonna come over and see it? Did you pick one out?"

"Not yet. You got any advice on what to look for?"

She tilted her head, giving his question earnest consideration. "Something extra, extra wide on bottom so lots of presents will fit under it."

He chuckled. "I'll keep that in mind." He rose, extending a hand toward the blond man. "You must be Steve Miller. Justin Cade. Nice to meet you."

"Ah." The man shook his hand. "*The* Justin Cade? I've heard a lot about you."

"You have?" Elisabeth looked startled. Apparently, she hadn't been the one volunteering information about him.

"All day while you were at work," Steven confirmed. "Did you know that Justin can imitate the voice of every single character on SpongeBob SquarePants? Alas, the best I can do is a passable 'ruh-roh' from Scooby Doo."

Justin laughed, liking the guy despite himself.

"It was nice to see you," Elisabeth said, "but we were just leaving. Good luck finding—"

"Leaving?" Kaylee wailed. "We haven't even got hot chocolate. You promised. And Justin doesn't have a tree. He needs our help picking a tree."

Steven was glancing at the little girl with alarm. Justin recognized some of the same trepidation he'd experienced the other day, when Kaylee had almost started crying and he hadn't known what to do.

"Don't you want my help?" Kaylee asked Justin. "I'm very good at picking trees."

"I… Of course I *want* your help," Justin said, not meeting Elisabeth's gaze, "but I can manage on my own if you have to go."

Steven lowered his voice. "Elisabeth, could I speak with you for a minute?"

"I'll keep an eye on Kaylee," Justin promised, waving them to the side. He valiantly ignored the temptation to eavesdrop. In part because Kaylee's animated chatter made it impossible.

"Wanna go throw snowballs?" she asked.

"I think we're supposed to stay in the tent. Patience. They'll be right back."

She made a face. "I was stuck inside all day. I like *outside.*"

Her conviction made him laugh. "Me, too, kiddo. That's why I have the best job in the world. I get to spend a lot of it outside."

"Steven has a boring job," she complained. "He was babysitting me, but he sat at the computer all day."

"You have to give him a chance," Justin told her. "He seems nice."

She twisted her mouth into a contemplative scowl. "He let me play a video game. But it was too hard."

"We may have a solution," Elisabeth said, rejoining them. "If Justin is willing to give Kaylee and me a ride home."

Steven's tone was apologetic. "My company is about to roll out a new version of our software, and there are still bugs. I hate to work while I'm visiting Elisabeth, but—"

"Hey, I'm the one who worked all day while you watched Kaylee," she reminded him with a smile. "Teamwork."

He kissed her on the cheek. "You're the best. Justin, what do you say? Any chance you could give the girls a lift?"

"Please!" Kaylee begged.

Looking into her big brown eyes, he knew there was no way he could refuse. "No problem. Now, what's this I hear about hot chocolate?"

He let Kaylee drag him toward the line at the concessions table while Elisabeth and Steven said goodbye. It only took a moment or two before Elisabeth fell into step with him.

"Elisabeth, can we get a cookie with our hot chocolate?" Kaylee asked.

"Okay, but only because it's the holiday season. And no dessert after dinner tonight," Elisabeth warned. "This is it for the day."

Undisturbed by thoughts of the dessertless future, Kaylee skipped ahead to check out the cookie selection and stood at the front of the line talking to a pigtailed girl she seemed to recognize.

Elisabeth's shoulders slumped. "This was probably a mistake."

"What, her inevitable sugar rush? Don't worry. Colin and I never paid enough attention to nutrition, and Arden turned out great. She willingly eats vegetables all the time."

"I meant staying here with you. Steven thought it would earn him points with Kaylee, but they're having a difficult enough time as it is. How's she supposed to bond with him while he's at my place and you're here being charming?"

He grinned. "You think I'm charming?"

"No. But I can see how a six-year-old might make that mistake."

"Ouch. I don't remember you being this mean."

"With as many women as you date," she said matter-of-factly, "I'm amazed you remember me at all. Do you have some kind of spreadsheet to keep track of us?"

It was on the tip of his tongue to tell her she wasn't like any of the others, that she'd been special. But what good would that do? Part of her distinction was how uncomfortable she'd made him. She would forever be off-limits to him even if she weren't engaged to be married.

Her mouth rounded in a surprised O. "You're hurt."

"Because you insinuated I'm a man-ho? No worries, my skin's thicker than that. Arden says horrible things to me all the time."

"Your cheek," she clarified. "It's hurt. Physically, literally. Injured."

"Oh, that." He raised a hand and pressed below his cheekbone, wincing. There would definitely be a bruise there. "Battle wounds from rescuing a damsel in distress. She—"

"Spare me any details of how she offered to kiss it all better," Elisabeth said, her tone withering.

There was an awful lot of disdain in her voice for someone who shouldn't care about his love life. Could she possibly be jealous? Of course not. Just as *he* was not bitter about her becoming Mrs. Elisabeth Miller.

"You misunderstand," he said. "The damsel in question was twelve. There was some flailing—she caught me with both an arm and a ski—but the physical pain wasn't nearly as bad as the loss of hearing she probably caused. Do all preteen girls shriek like banshees?"

At that, Elisabeth smiled. "I have news for you, it's not just the tweens. I was in Denver for Kaylee's fifth birthday. She was overstimulated and overtired and threw an epic fit. I thought my ears would actually start bleeding."

"And now? Any tantrums since she moved in with you?"

"Not at first, but she's getting there."

"Why do you sound like tantrums would be progress?"

"In some ways, it would be a relief. I think all normal kids throw one or two. Lord knows Lina did. But when Kaylee first moved in with me… She was far too solemn for a child her age. And painfully tentative, as if she was afraid I'd make her leave if she did anything wrong. She needs to know this is permanent, that I'll love her no matter what."

Her tone was fiercely maternal. She made a damn good mother, even if she'd only been on the job for a few months.

Did her fiancé have what it took to be an equally

capable father? And what kind of husband would he make? The man seemed like a decent, likable guy, but what was with that kiss on Elisabeth's cheek? Obviously, they weren't going to make out in front of Kaylee and a bunch of Christmas-tree enthusiasts, but shouldn't there be *some* chemistry between them? Justin knew firsthand how passionate Elisabeth could be.

"Stevie wasn't what I expected," he said.

"Don't call him 'Stevie.' It's patronizing."

"Can I call him Maurice?" he teased. "Or how about 'the space cowboy'? From 'The Joker'? Oh, come on, that was funny."

Kaylee bounced back toward them, waving goodbye to the girl with pigtails. "That was Marissa. She's in the class next to mine. Marissa's mom says maybe I can come to their house after Christmas. They have a rabbit!"

"That sounds like fun," Elisabeth said, but Justin noticed the concern in her eyes. Was she worried about Kaylee finally starting to make friends just as the time came to leave Cielo Peak?

They moved to the front of the line, ordering three cocoas with extra marshmallows. As he stirred his, he felt Elisabeth's gaze on him and caught her staring at his cheek again.

"Don't worry," he told her. "It looks worse than it is."

"I forget sometimes how dangerous your job can be," she admitted. "You take care of yourself out there, okay?"

"Always." As he'd demonstrated when he broke up with her, looking out for himself was what he did best.

ELISABETH'S RESERVATIONS ABOUT staying with Justin at the tree farm were no match for Kaylee's delighted giggles as the girl darted between scotch pines and blue spruces. Justin played "Marco Polo" with her, pretending not to know exactly which row she was in until she jumped out to surprise him, eliciting comical shrieks.

It was bittersweet to watch them together. He was so damn good with her. *Probably because he himself is a big kid at heart.* She had to remind herself that knowing how to have fun wasn't the same thing as being reliable. There was a man back at her place who would never let her down or break her heart.

"Okay, you two, you seem to have forgotten why we're here. Justin needs a tree," she reminded Kaylee. "Any suggestions?"

The girl offered opinions ranging from "that one might make Santa sneeze" to "this one's got a bald spot, like our principal."

Justin made a show of weighing her sage advice as he steered her away from any tree over four feet. "My house isn't very big, so I need a small one. Those are the best, anyway, because it's easy to reach the top."

"We always had an angel at the top of our tree," Kaylee said shyly. "The angel's pretty, but not as cute as my teddy bear snowman. That's my favorite of all."

Elisabeth inhaled sharply, cursing her lack of foresight, and Justin met her gaze over the top of Kaylee's head. Michelle's Christmas decorations were amid the many boxes stacked in a storage unit in Denver. Elisabeth had brought all of Kaylee's belongings with them and sold Michelle's bigger pieces of furniture. But there were tons of items Elisabeth hadn't been able to face.

She'd planned to sort through it all with Kaylee when the girl was older.

They were supposed to decorate their tree tonight, their first together as a family, and she suddenly suspected that Kaylee wasn't going to be very impressed. Throughout Elisabeth's childhood, the Christmas trees had always been gaudy affairs, strewn with a mishmash of school pictures in painted macaroni frames, funky knit snowmen made by Grandma Donnelly and all of Lina's favorite ornaments clumped together in one group.

Once she moved out on her own, Elisabeth was free to have an elegant, color-coordinated tree. All of her ornaments were blue and silver, many of them crystal and not very kid-friendly. She didn't even have an angel. She used a three-tiered Waterford topper made of blown glass. It was exquisite, but it was no teddy bear snowman.

"I think I saw some ornaments for sale in the tent," Justin said. "Maybe you could pick one out before we go, a souvenir from Cielo Peak."

"What's a 'souvenir?'" Kaylee asked.

"An item that helps you remember special places or events," Elisabeth explained.

The little girl looked indignant. "I would never forget Cielo Peak! It's my home."

Not for long. Elisabeth bit her lip, torn between reminding Kaylee that they had lots of new, wonderful things to look forward to in California and simply letting her enjoy the moment. It was wonderful to see her smiling.

"Snowball fight!" Justin called his announcement

at the same time he lobbed a ball in Elisabeth's direction. It thudded against her shoulder, distracting Kaylee's attention and putting an end to Elisabeth's internal struggle. For the moment, anyway.

Elisabeth bent to pack some snow between her gloves, making Kaylee laugh with her vows of retaliation.

But the impromptu snow battle highlighted why Justin Cade had never been the right man for her. He excelled at temporary distractions, not long-term solutions. When relationships got too intense for him, he slipped away faster than a snowball would melt in the summer sun. Kaylee might be too young to understand that, but it was Elisabeth's job to remember it for both their sakes.

Chapter Six

When Elisabeth arrived at Arden's studio Saturday morning, she expected to encounter a few reminders of Justin—after all, he was Arden's brother. But she hadn't been expecting to encounter Justin himself. She drew up short in the doorway, sucking in her breath. *You have* got *to be kidding me.*

He smiled ruefully over the head of the infant he held against his shoulder. "I'm not stalking you, I swear."

"Aren't you supposed to be at work?" she asked, finally remembering to move so that Kaylee and Steven could also come in from the cold.

"I've got an odd shift today. Don't go in until after lunch since I'll be working abnormally late." He reached down to tousle Kaylee's curls when she hugged him. "I'm teaching a first aid class around seven and leading a moonlight snowshoe tour. Meanwhile, Arden had a last-minute change of child-care plans so I agreed to meet her here and take my gorgeous niece off her hands for a few hours."

"He's a lifesaver," his sister added. She stood a few feet away, stirring a packet of creamer into a mug of coffee. "My normal weekend sitter is a schoolteacher. She's taking advantage of the two-week vacation to visit some cousins in Texas. My backup sitter is Jill Dennis, but she called this morning to say she was coming down with a bad cold. I couldn't risk leaving Hope with someone who's sick." There was a note of anxious apology in her voice, as if she worried her clients would think her unprofessional for having her baby at the studio.

"Of course you couldn't let her stay with someone who's ill," Elisabeth agreed promptly. Although she and Arden were, regrettably, not as close as they'd once been, she'd heard about Hope's first few days spent in a special incubator. She could only imagine how protective Arden must be of her child.

Noting the garment bag draped over Steven's arm and the small duffel he carried with accessories for varying outfits, Arden pointed him toward the changing room. "You can put those in there. There are already hangers on the rod if you need them, so everything stays unwrinkled and camera-ready."

"Can I hold the baby?" Kaylee asked, sticking both arms straight out in front of her.

Justin lowered his voice to a friendly, confidential tone, as if he were sharing an important secret. "I'd better hold on to her—I've almost got her to sleep. You wouldn't believe what a *pain* she is when she doesn't get her naps. I mean, she's crankier than Chef Bates when someone rearranges any of the supplies in his walk-in pantry."

Kaylee giggled, and Justin bent his legs so that he was closer to her height—albeit, not by much.

"Here," he whispered. "This way you can get a better look at her. Just remember, no touching. And keep your voice soft like mine."

"So she'll fall asleep," Kaylee agreed. "And not be a pain."

Elisabeth couldn't help creeping forward for a closer look of her own. The infant was tiny, bundled in a fuzzy blanket, her head covered in an adorable hat that looked like a polar bear face. Beneath the baby's sleepy eyelids, Elisabeth glimpsed the same blue-green color of Justin's eyes. *She could pass for his daughter.* It was a bittersweet thought, imagining him cradling a child of his own against his broad chest. He looked like such a natural with his niece, but Elisabeth knew he had no intentions of ever becoming a father.

Although he made jokes about being "the shallow Cade," she suspected his aversion to building a family came from losing loved ones. Would he ever change? Would sufficient time pass for him to one day overcome his emotional baggage? Or would he perhaps meet a woman he cared for enough to face his fears?

Whether it happened or not, she wouldn't be around to see it. She'd be in California, embracing her future. Grateful she'd met a man dependable enough to offer her that future, she flashed a warm smile over her shoulder at Steven, who was being pretty gracious about running into Elisabeth's ex for the second time in two days. He'd confirmed after Kaylee went to bed last night that Elisabeth and Justin had once dated, but he hadn't seemed threatened by it. *And why should he be?* It was Steven's ring she was wearing. Justin was the distant past.

Although, he sure seemed to be popping up a lot in her present.

Elisabeth stepped forward to make introductions. "Arden, this is my fiancé, Steven Miller." Behind her, Justin began humming to the baby. Elisabeth assumed it was a lullaby but a moment later, as she accepted Arden's offer of coffee, she identified the tune as "Fly Like An Eagle." She shot him an unamused glance, which he returned with a phony expression of boyish innocence.

Smart-ass. But she caught herself fighting a grin as she turned back around.

"Did you two have something particular in mind for your pictures?" Arden was asking. "I have standard backgrounds and props, and we can try lots of different poses then see what looks best in the proofs. But some couples bring in meaningful items or request settings uniquely personal to them."

"We don't have anything like that." Elisabeth blurted her answer without thought. It was only after she'd spoken that she worried she'd made them sound like a dull couple. There were obviously moments and symbols of personal significance for them, she just couldn't think of one off the top of her head. "Our main request is that you do a couple of shots that also include Kaylee. We'll probably use one with just us as the official engagement photo, but we're going to be a family. We wanted some portraits of all three of us."

Arden nodded. "If you haven't finished your Christmas shopping, a nice framed photo of the three of you could make a great gift for relatives."

Typically, Elisabeth was done buying gifts by the

end of November. This year—with Kaylee in her life—was a bit different, but there was already a neat stack of family presents in her closet waiting to be wrapped while she listened to her carol playlist or watched *White Christmas*. In light of Arden's question about special mementos, Elisabeth was suddenly second-guessing her high-tech purchases for Steven, including a messenger bag charging station for all his electronic devices. Should she have picked out something with more emotional significance?

She'd never been particularly adept at the sappy stuff. Lacking her sister's creative flair, Elisabeth's forte was practicality. Back when she'd been dating Justin, she'd struggled with what to get him for his birthday. After two weeks of waffling between ski gear or a gift card, she'd given in to a silly whim and presented him with a book of erotic redeemable coupons. Not a groundbreaking gift in terms of originality, but he'd reacted with a wickedly appreciative smile. *"Just what I always wanted. How'd you know?"*

She wasn't sure they'd made it through the whole book before he ended their relationship, but while it lasted, it was difficult to say which of them had enjoyed his present more. The biggest downside had been not anticipating the moment when Patti Donnelly asked at the dining room table, "What did you get him, dear?" Elisabeth's cheeks had burned hotter than the candles on the cake.

"Okay, Arden." The sound of Justin's rumbling baritone snapped Elisabeth out of her memories. He was buckling the baby into the infant car seat that doubled as a carrier. "We already put the base for the seat in my SUV, I've got her feeding schedule, her blanket, the insanely heavy diaper bag, the folding travel crib, a partridge and a pear tree. If that's everything, I'm heading out."

Kaylee's bottom lip, much like the Grinch's heart, grew three sizes. "You're going already? Can I go with you?"

While he'd been busy gathering baby gear, Justin had apparently missed the part about Kaylee being in the pictures. "Want me to get her out from underfoot for a couple of hours?" he asked Elisabeth. He no doubt thought he was doing them a favor, keeping the girl occupied while they had their photo shoot. "I could use an assistant babysitter."

Steven met her gaze. "You did say you wanted to run some wedding errands after. I don't mind if she stays with Justin. If he doesn't mind waiting a few minutes so Arden can take the pictures with her first?"

Justin shrugged in agreement, and Kaylee beamed so brightly that pictures of her would probably come out overexposed. Elisabeth was the only person in the room who didn't seem delighted with the arrangement. It wasn't that she minded Justin looking after Kaylee. It would be much easier to concentrate on pricing at the bakery and florist without a six-year-old underfoot, but… Was Steven avoiding the little girl? He sometimes seemed to be at a loss for what to say to her, which she understood. He was an only child without a lot of experience with kids. But if they were going to be married, he couldn't avoid Elisabeth's daughter forever.

That wasn't a discussion for the lobby of Arden's studio, however.

"Thank you," she told Justin. "You've made her day. Again."

"I'm glad. I've always liked her." He watched fondly as Kaylee executed happy twirls around the reception area, her blue-and-green plaid skirt billowing out over her leggings. "It was horrible what she and her mother went through. Not that I met Michelle, but I've seen what cancer does. And when Kaylee moved here…"

She waited, curious what he would say.

"Never mind. You should be getting ready for your close-up, not wasting time with me."

She retreated to check her makeup and straighten Kaylee's blue hair bow, but his casual words stayed with her. He'd said "wasting time." There had been a point after their breakup when she'd wondered if the months with him *had* been a waste. Why had she invested so much in a relationship that a more intelligent woman might have seen was doomed from their first date? Yet, she didn't think she'd ever truly loved a man until Justin. There'd been crushes, of course, and boyfriends about whom she'd cared deeply. But he had been different. Before him, she'd never once rolled over in the morning and thought, *That's the face I want to wake up to for the rest of my life.* Even though their relationship hadn't worked out, maybe he'd opened her up to new possibilities, new depths of feeling.

Her time with Justin had been many things—unexpected, adventurous, infuriating, arousing and ultimately wrenching. But it hadn't been a waste.

JUSTIN FOUND HIMSELF half wishing that baby Hope would wake up and cry. At least then, he could walk with her, patting her back and feeling useful. While she slept peacefully in the carrier, he had nothing to do but watch and wait. He looked on while Arden and Elisabeth admired each other's engagement rings, and he had a surreal moment where it felt as if everyone around him were getting married. In reality, he only knew of the two couples, but since he was in the room with one and a half of those couples, it still left him strangely isolated.

Then Arden got the trio arranged in front of a formal background, and Justin had to admit the future Miller family looked good together. They'd color-coordinated in a way that was unifying but not so identical that it created a disturbing Stepford effect. Steven's tie was the same color blue as the sweater beneath Elisabeth's blazer, highlighting the blue in Kaylee's print dress. Justin had to glance away. The tableau they made, smiling and nestled together, was too much. Too taunting, too treacherous.

Looking at them would beguile most anyone into daydreams about white picket fences and silver anniversaries, but that wasn't the whole story, was it? He remembered quite well how happy his parents had looked together. And how losing Rebecca Cade had devastated his father. As far as Justin was concerned, the man had died of a broken heart. After Rebecca's death, Justin's dad sank into depression and a series of seemingly unrelated maladies until his heart failed. For the final years of his life, the man had been more a ghost of himself than an actual father. And now there was Colin....

Justin couldn't imagine the hell Colin had endured

when he lost his wife and young son; he only knew that since then, his brother had gone renegade. He'd given up his job, his home and all but a few remaining ties to his brother and sister. Thinking of how different Colin had become, how bitter, Justin forced himself to look back at Elisabeth. Despite the smiles beaming at the camera, was there anything on the other side of his sister's lens that wholly justified the emotional risk?

Arden worked quickly, changing sets and poses while respecting her clients' time. "I think I've got some great shots of the three of you," she told Elisabeth, "if you want to release Kaylee and focus on the engagement pictures."

"Sounds good." Elisabeth hugged Kaylee and admonished her to behave. Then she turned to Justin. "I promise we'll try to get through our errands quickly. I don't want to take advantage of your generosity. Do you want to meet us somewhere, or should I just pick her up at your place?"

"My place is fine."

She averted her gaze, and he wondered if she recalled the last time she was there, after his birthday. They'd had a hell of a night that lasted into early morning. She'd been the most beautiful woman he'd ever seen, dawn bathing her naked skin as she drifted to sleep in his bed, her red-gold hair fanned across the pillow in a near match for the sun's rays. As he'd watched her, it felt as if something had cracked inside him.

"I should change," she said after an awkward pause. "See you both later."

Justin helped bundle Kaylee into her jacket, then picked up the baby carrier. They were on their way to his SUV when the door to the studio flew open behind them.

"We forgot the booster seat," Elisabeth called, chasing after them in such a hurry she hadn't even bothered with a jacket. She looked stunning in a wraparound black dress. Apparently, she'd wanted something more sophisticated for the engagement photos than the wholesome family portrait. It was a deceptively simple garment—hanging in a closet, it might even have looked boring. But molded to her lush curves, it was silky, sinful temptation.

They transferred Kaylee's seat to his SUV, and Justin was momentarily disoriented, as if he'd hit his head hard. Or fallen into an alternate dimension. He was the most confirmed bachelor and least likely family man in all of Cielo Peak. So why was he pulling out of the parking lot with two adorable little girls buckled into the back of his vehicle like he was a freaking soccer mom?

During the drive to his house, snow began to fall. There was already plenty of accumulation on the ground, but he never got tired of the untouched magic of brand-new snow, blanketing over ruts and muddy patches.

"Can we make a snowman?" Kaylee asked as they pulled into his driveway.

"Not today, kiddo. We should stay inside with Hope in case she wakes up. But I have an idea. I haven't started decorating my tree yet. Want to help?" After getting home yesterday evening with his impulsive purchase, he'd discovered that he owned exactly three ornaments.

There was a snowboarding Santa in a pair of goggles; Trey Grainger's wife had bought them in bulk last year and given one to each of the eighty patrollers. Then there was a promotional ornament that had come free with a six-pack of soda at some point. Finally, there were two cartoonish cats embracing under a sprig of mistletoe, a memento from the month he'd dated a waitress named Kitty.

Even though he'd deliberately picked a small tree, he was going to need more than three meager ornaments. He'd knocked off a few of the evergreen needles while trying to get the tree situated on a coffee table, and he didn't own a proper tree stand, so he'd improvised. As a result, the tree was leaning slightly to the left. It was a little like Charlie Brown's tree. No, that wasn't true—it was like another, sadder tree that *aspired* to be half as grand as Chuck's.

She crossed her arms over her chest. "Are all *your* decorations breakful, too?"

"You mean breakable? Like glass and stuff?"

She bobbed her head in affirmation. "I'm not allowed to touch those kind."

"Good news, I don't have any breakable ornaments. In fact, you're looking at all my decorations."

"Don't you know where the stores are?" she asked, clearly aghast that he couldn't figure out how to buy more.

"Yes, but I thought we could make some ornaments. Like out of popcorn and stuff."

"I like popcorn."

"Then we're in business." Just as soon as he located the needle and thread he was about 80 percent sure he owned. He had a dim recollection of buying a kit to replace a button before he'd decided he didn't like that particular shirt enough to bother.

The baby stayed asleep while he microwaved two bags of popcorn, burning one of them slightly. He got the popcorn started so that Kaylee didn't accidentally stab herself with the business end of the needle, then let her slide the pieces down the string. She also ate some of the would-be decorations, but he told himself that at least popcorn had no sugar. As they worked, he remembered Arden once making a chain of paper loops. Since he didn't have any construction paper, he brought Kaylee a stack of his *Sports Illustrated* magazines. He showed her how to look for colorful pictures and tear the page into strips.

Soon after that, Hope woke, loudly demanding a bottle. Justin settled into a chair with her and watched as Kaylee glued strips of varying width into lopsided circles. Truth be told, he thought more of the glue was getting on her than on the chain, but at least she was enjoying herself.

As soon as they hung the makeshift decorations, however, Kaylee frowned at him. "You don't have any lights. Christmas trees need lights. It's a rule."

"A rule, huh?" Did he own lights? He couldn't recall the last time he'd done any holiday decorating beyond a novelty wreath on his front door, but surely somewhere... He had a sudden brainstorm. Back in October, his sister's best friend had drafted him to help with the high school's haunted house fund-raiser. He still had a few strings of lights in a miscellaneous box in the garage.

Situating Hope in the supportive baby sling he'd found in her bag, he headed into the garage. He returned with one string of purple bats and another of orange pumpkins. "These are the best I could do," he told Kaylee. "A little unorthodox, but they do light up when you plug them in."

Now his crooked tree, which was previously decked in three mismatched ornaments, also bore a popcorn garland, a paper chain soggy with glue and orange-and-purple Halloween lights. *Yeah, that's progress.*

"Guess it doesn't look much like the one you have at home, does it, kiddo?"

"Nuh-uh." She stared up at him, brown eyes full of something perilously close to hero worship. "Yours is *way* better."

Elisabeth should be filled with satisfaction. In a short period of time, she and Steven had accomplished a lot, crossing a number of items off their to-do list. But she couldn't shake her nagging sense of unease. It grew worse the closer they got to Justin's house.

Even the clicking of her blinker as she waited to turn left set her nerves on edge. "Steven, can I tell you something?"

He glanced up immediately from whatever he'd been reading on his cell phone. "Of course. You know I'm always here to listen."

That was true. She'd desperately needed someone to talk to after Michelle died, and Steven had been amazing. He'd been going through a difficult time at work and had questioned whether to push through it in hopes of something bigger at the company or take his chances elsewhere. They'd made each other laugh at the ends of stressful days and given each other plenty of advice.

"We've been bumping into Justin a lot, and I'm feeling guilty because there's something I haven't mentioned."

He waited, not impatient or suspicious, but encouraging.

"The day you got here, I met Justin for lunch to ask about his sister taking our pictures, and afterward—" She broke off, the admission seeming silly now that she put it into words. "He almost kissed me."

"Almost? But didn't? I suppose that's understandable. You're a beautiful woman, and the two of you have history."

"You aren't mad?" Deep down, she'd known he wouldn't be, but she supposed she'd been hoping for *some* kind of reaction.

"There's no reason. Even if he'd gone through with it, you would have pushed him away." He squeezed her hand affectionately. "I trust you. You'd never betray me."

"I feel the same way about you." There was a lot of mutual respect and friendship in this car. But was that enough for a lifetime?

Damn it. A week ago, she'd felt confident in her decision to marry Steven. Was she simply experiencing the same, run-of-the-mill cold feet all brides experienced from time to time, or were her misgivings serious enough to explore further?

A third, more embarrassing possibility was that her recent close encounters with Justin were throwing her emotional barometer out of whack. Perhaps she hadn't done herself any favors by diligently avoiding him after their breakup. Granted, Cielo Peak's size made it difficult to cut another resident completely from one's life, but by spending all her time at the lodge and in Justin-free zones like the elementary school and pediatrician's office, she'd managed pretty well. Unfortunately, all that avoidance hadn't given her the opportunity for closure, the chance to prove to herself that she was completely over him.

Well, you have the chance now. Take it.

She parked in front of his house and unbuckled her seat belt. "Are you coming in with me, or would you rather wait here?"

He chuckled. "I told you, I trust you. I'm not worried about you being alone with him for two minutes while I check email."

There was a formal front door, but Justin discouraged people from using it because the porch steps were rickety. Not to mention, they were currently covered in snow and ice. She walked to the side of the house, to the door beneath the carport. She could hear the low drone of a television inside, paired with Justin's deep, muffled voice and Kaylee's higher-pitched laugh. It occurred to Elisabeth that Kaylee might not be happy to see her since it meant playtime was over.

But the little girl was all smiles as she ducked under Justin's arm and scrambled to greet Elisabeth. "We had *so much fun!*" Technically, her voice was too soft to qualify as an actual squeal, but what she lacked in volume she made up for with intensity. "Justin has the best tree ever. Come see!"

They crossed through the kitchen and into the living room. Kaylee gestured toward the tree with a proud "ta-da!"

Elisabeth gaped. "Is that…Silly String clumped around the middle part? The stuff you spray out of cans?"

"Well, I didn't have any tinsel," Justin said as if that explained the sticky strands of neon plastic.

"And those are…" Not believing her eyes, she leaned in for a closer look.

"Bats!" Kaylee chirped. "Aren't they *awesome?*"

Elisabeth ruffled the girl's hair. "I can honestly say, I've never seen a Christmas tree like it." Halloween lights, popcorn—some of it burned—and glossy paper loops that featured fragmented images of basketballs and a golf course. It was like something from a Tim Burton film, by way of ESPN. "Steven's waiting in the car. I'm sure he'll want to hear all about the tree, too. You ready to go?"

"Need my shoes," Kaylee said, zipping around the corner to collect them.

"She's a cute kid," Justin commented.

A kid who's already way too attached to you. "Thank you again. We should get going. Steven and I knocked a few tasks off our list but still have a lot to do."

"A little picking and grinning, some loving and sinning?" His deadpan expression was at odds with his singsong delivery.

She glared. "Enough with the Steve Miller Band jokes."

"One more?" he pleaded, his eyes twinkling unrepentantly. "I had a good one for 'Take the Money and Run.'"

Fitting. Who knew more about running than Justin? He'd been the only guy she'd ever told "I love you" without the other person saying it first. And he'd bolted like he was trying to outrun a coming apocalypse.

She spun on her heel, ready to collect her kid and get the hell out of Justin's house. There were too many memories here—breathless, pulse-pounding memories.

Justin followed. "I don't know when Steven leaves town, but if your mom or sister can babysit some night, you two should look into one of these moonlight tours. They're pretty romantic. Just your cup of tea."

"Maybe you're not a very good judge of what my cup is. Most people wouldn't call me a romantic."

"Most people don't know you like I do."

At one time, he certainly had known her—she'd opened up to him in ways she never had to anyone else. And he'd rejected her. She bent down to button Kaylee's coat, then opened the door, glad to be leaving. But she stopped two steps down the sidewalk, turning back to where Justin filled the doorway.

"You *knew* me," she stressed. "Past tense. You can't assume I'm the same person I was."

The real question was, as she adapted to becoming a parent and tried to plan a future she was questioning more and more, did *she* know who she was?

Chapter Seven

As far as Justin was concerned, a shopping mall three days before Christmas was on par with the ninth circle of hell. *What am I doing here?* But the obvious answer to that question stood next to him in the serpentine line to meet Santa Claus. Arden had asked him to come with her after work, and it was damn near impossible to refuse his sister. He had, however, tried to throw Garrett under the bus by asking if she wouldn't rather wait until her fiancé got to town to take Hope for her inaugural Santa picture.

"I think this will make a nice surprise for him," she'd insisted. "Besides, it will be evening by the time he gets into town tomorrow. He'll be hungry and tired from the drive. We probably wouldn't be able to get here until Tuesday, and taking the baby to the mall on Christmas Eve—are you crazy?"

But going on the evening of December twenty-second, apparently, was completely sane in her book.

He understood why she'd delayed this long. Although Santa had taken up his post at the mall weeks ago, Arden had wanted to wait until the baby was older and stronger before bringing Hope to such a public place. Even now, she insisted that Santa would not be putting his "germ-ridden gloves" on her child. Instead, Arden would hold the baby in the photo and frame a copy to give Garrett on Christmas Eve.

Justin bounced restlessly on the balls of his feet. "Don't take this as a complaint—you know I'd do anything for you and Hope—but is this line even moving? I feel like we've been here for hours." They'd talked about grabbing a quick dinner in the food court afterward, but at the rate they were going, the mall would close before they made their way to the front.

"It hasn't been that long," Arden said. But she stole a glance at her watch and frowned. Luckily, Hope was asleep in her bassinet-style stroller, oblivious to the cacophony around her or the interminable wait.

Justin envied her serenity. To a guy who spent so much time in the great outdoors, the vast blue sky above him and a slope of groomed powder stretched before him, being stuck in the mall was starting to feel like being buried alive—along with a couple hundred other people. If the walls weren't exactly closing in on him, the crowd certainly was.

He was surrounded by families and youngsters of all types. Some of the more obnoxious kids seemed to view Santa as similar to a hostage negotiator, and they impatiently waited to present him with a list of demands. Other children, especially in the under-five demographic, were shrieking in terror, understandably scared of a large man who stole into homes while everyone slept. It probably didn't help that adults had filled impressionable heads with stories of an omniscient North Pole spy who watches kids while they're sleeping *and* while they're awake. Elsewhere in the mob, siblings squabbled while harried mothers threatened, "If you don't cool it, right now, we are going home!" Was it wrong that Justin was mentally egging on the juvenile delinquents—at least, the ones in front of him? Anyone who exited the line got Arden and Hope one spot closer.

But it wasn't the noise of crying and bickering that left him itchy and uncomfortable in his own skin. The happy families were the hardest to take. Mothers and fathers grinned affectionately at each other over the heads of tykes in cute holiday sweaters and bright green dresses. A man stood with his arms around a woman, pressing a quick kiss to the nape of her neck, while identical twin boys burbled happily in their double-stroller.

Justin looked away, desperate to think about something else. "I remember doing this with you," he heard himself say. "Your first trip to see Santa, I mean."

"You do?" Arden smiled up at him. Family anecdotes about her infancy were rare. Neither of their parents had survived to share the stories. Justin and Colin, who had been in elementary school and middle school, had been paying more attention to preteen girls than their bald, drooling baby sister. They'd loved Arden, no mistake, but it had never occurred to them to take special note of her first word or how she learned to walk.

"Colin and I didn't want to go, not at first. We were too old for this kind of thing. And much too cool."

"Naturally."

"But Mom insisted. She loved this time of year. She volunteered at the local food pantry and spearheaded toy drives, anything to help share her joy with others. She'd crank up the Christmas carols and sing along while she cooked all our annual favorites. And the woman, she could *not* sing. I mean, neighborhood dogs would start howling. But she always got us to join in anyway." None of them had much range to speak of, although Colin's deep voice was surprisingly rich and pleasant when he sang. "She had the three guys in her life wrapped around her finger. She was a bit like you when it came to persuading people to do what she wanted."

He paused, looking around pointedly.

Arden gave him an impish smile and motioned for him to carry on with his tale.

"Anyway, Mom said that a baby only gets one first picture with Santa, and she wanted both of your brothers to be in the shot with you. While we were in line, Colin turned bright red. A girl from his class walked out of a nearby store with her mother, and Colin was mortified. But the girl noticed you, an adorable chubby-cheeked six-month-old, and started fawning all over you. She asked Mom point-blank to call her if she ever needed a babysitter, and a month or so later, I think that girl was Colin's first kiss."

Arden rolled her eyes. "So your sentimental holiday story ended up being about how one of my brothers used to me to charm a girl and ultimately make out with her?"

"Hey, you want heartwarming, go to Hallmark. Sentiment isn't my specialty." Not that he was unaffected by the reminiscing. "After Mom got sick, I was so damn grateful for that afternoon and others like it—

instances when I didn't think I wanted to be there but had no idea that our time together was limited. Now, I'm thankful for that twenty minutes we stood in line, joking with each other, having contests to see which of us could make you laugh first, teasing Colin about a pretty classmate... I'm sorry you didn't have more of those days, with our family still intact."

Eyes bright, she leaned over to hug him. "You and Colin have been my family. I couldn't have asked for better brothers." She sighed. "I don't suppose you've heard from him?"

"We've played phone tag. I think he's working pretty erratic hours." *And that he's avoiding us.* "He assured me in his last message that he will absolutely be here for Christmas, but I don't have specifics. He won't let you down, Arden. No worries, okay?"

"No worries." Her emotion-clogged tone clashed with the carefree words. Turning her head, she surreptitiously wiped at the tears she seemed to think he couldn't see.

As a family who'd already had their turn with Santa passed by on the outside of the velvet ropes, Arden gasped indignantly. "Did you see the picture she was carrying? It was off-center, and the lighting was completely wrong."

He laughed. "I should have known better than to accompany a professional photographer to let someone else take her picture. Is this like that saying about doctors making the worst patients?"

"I'm not being difficult," she said defensively.

"Never said you were, sis."

"It's not wrong to have standards and pride in my

work." She narrowed her eyes as if daring him to correct her.

Ha! He wasn't stupid.

"You know, it isn't too late to scrap this plan," he told her. "We could go to your studio. I know a few older ski bums who could let me borrow a red suit and some padding. You can take the high-quality portrait Garrett and Hope deserve."

She poked him in the ribs. "You're just looking for an excuse to leave."

"Being here is freaking me out," he admitted, wondering if he could explain his sudden onset of claustrophobia in a way that would make sense to her.

"This freaks you out?" she echoed. "This? Correct me if I'm wrong, but didn't you have dawn patrol this morning where you hiked through the mountains with several pounds of *dynamite* strapped to your back?"

"Carefully stowed in my backpack, yes. I've had extensive training and years of practice for doing avalanche prevention." After heavy snowfalls, such as the town had experienced late last night, a patrol often went out to do avalanche prevention. The blasting created controlled avalanches, rather than waiting for an unsuspecting tourist to trigger a slab. Although there hadn't been much accumulation today, they were expecting another front to move in, dropping more snow tonight and possibly bringing about blizzard conditions. Patrollers knew that "blizzard" didn't just mean a lot of the white stuff, it referred to dangerously high winds and a serious lack of visibility.

"Guess I was so busy learning about safety on the

mountain," he said, "that I missed the sessions on how to survive the mall during Yuletide."

"Take heart," Arden told him. "I think we've moved up two places in the past ten minutes."

"If it keeps up like this, we'll reach the front just in time for her to have her picture taken with the Easter Bunny," he quipped. "Are you sure I can't convince you to go to your studio?"

"Quite. As you pointed out in your story about me, a baby's first Santa photo is a rite of passage. Besides, practically every photo I've given Garrett of her so far has been taken by me. This will be a nice change of pace. But speaking of my studio, Elisabeth called yesterday evening. They were happy with the engagement photos."

"Was there ever any doubt?"

"Actually…" She pursed her lips. "Some of the takes were great, but there were others I was less pleased with. My job is more than technical proficiency with the equipment. I have to put my clients at ease, find the real them, so to speak."

"You're not going to get all New Agey on me and start talking about trying to capture people's auras on camera, are you?"

She ignored him. "I feel like maybe I didn't succeed in putting them at ease. A few of the pictures had a stilted quality where they didn't look like two people in love so much as two people who are supposed to look like they're in love, like models in a bridal magazine, if that makes any sense."

He didn't want to hear this. Elisabeth wasn't part of his life anymore. She'd moved on. It would be great if he could imagine her deliriously happy with the new man in her life. Justin had been riddled with guilt over hurting her, but as long as he knew she'd found someone better for her, he could tell himself he'd done the right thing. That it had worked out for the best. One door closing, windows opening and all that jazz.

"Justin, I spent time around you two while you were dating. I remember how she looked at you. She doesn't look at him the same way."

"Maybe that's because she's not the same person anymore." He parroted Elisabeth's words from yesterday to his sister. "Stop trying to read into it. And for heaven's sake, don't mention this to anyone else. The last thing clients want in a wedding photographer is someone casting a black cloud over the nuptials!"

"I wouldn't say this to anyone else. But don't you—"

"Hold that thought." He reached in his back pocket for his cell phone. *Saved by the ringtone.* He held it up so Arden could see the screen, too. "Hey, look who's calling. Colin. What's up, man?"

"Justin? I can barely hear you over the background noise. Where the hell are you? A riot?"

"Close enough. Hang on a sec." He muted the phone and asked Arden, "Mind if I abandon you for a few minutes? I'm going to look for a quieter corner to take this call."

"Tell him we miss him and I can't wait to see him."

"Will do."

Justin went toward the end of the mall where a new department store was being built. Since the coming store was still under construction, the corridor was currently a dead end. Few shoppers were around. There were distant sounds of power tools, but even those were melodious compared to the mingled tantrums, joyful shrieks and tattling in the Santa line.

"This better?" he asked Colin.

"Yeah."

He almost complained about Arden's dragging him to the mall for the Santa meet and greet, but stopped abruptly, recalling a picture of Colin's little boy that had once hung on Justin's fridge. Baby Hope was not his first niece or nephew. Justin had been an uncle in what felt like a former lifetime.

"How are you holding up?" he asked his older brother. Colin had been their rock, the one who'd held them together after their parents died. To witness him crumble was nerve-racking. Justin tried not to draw parallels between Colin and their late father, who'd withdrawn after losing his wife. Was his brother on a similar road to self-destruction?

Not that Colin was sitting around in a recliner, hiding from the world and passively declining. Far from it. He'd tossed away the large animal vet practice he'd built, sold his house and purchased a motorcycle which he drove at breakneck speeds. If he was going to self-destruct, he was being far more proactive about it.

"I'm glad to be out of Cielo Peak," Colin said candidly. "Easier to breathe when I'm not there."

"But you *are* coming back for Christmas?" Justin pressed. If his brother backed out now, Arden's head would explode.

"I'll be there. I'm a little surprised that you're the one who's been leaving me nagging voice mails, though. Christmas isn't really your thing."

"Very true. But when you skipped town, you left me in charge of looking after Arden. This means a lot to her. You have to be here." It wasn't as if Colin had a high-pressure office position and couldn't get the time off from work. He'd been drifting aimlessly doing ranching odd jobs based on contacts and references from his veterinarian days.

"I'll be there by noon on Christmas Eve. Can I crash at your place while I'm in town?"

"You even have to ask?"

"Didn't want to cramp your style. There've been periods of your life where you average a lot of overnight guests."

"Now is not one of those periods." It had been weeks since he'd even bought a woman a drink, much less brought a woman home.

"Losing your touch, bro?"

"I…" For a moment, Justin was tempted to resurrect the decades' old habit of confiding in his brother and asking for advice. The image of Elisabeth's face haunted him. She'd looked upset at his house yesterday. He didn't know how to interpret her assertion that she was no longer the same person she'd been six months ago. And now Arden was worried that Elisabeth lacked the emotion she'd felt for Justin.

A sudden, vibrant memory assailed him, of making love to Elisabeth on a warm summer night. He'd rolled her over, not paying enough attention to the mattress edge and nearly sent the both of them careening to the floor. She'd cracked up, laughing between her kisses, completely unselfconscious, uninhibited in both her passion and her humor. That moment had stuck with him for a long time afterward, making him grin inwardly when he heard a guy in town say that both Donnelly women were attractive but that Elisabeth was a lot more "buttoned-up." Justin had seen her unbuttoned. Had he done something to damage that, to extinguish that flame in her?

He hoped not. For her sake, he hoped that behind closed doors she was just as unexpectedly passionate with Steven—although he automatically recoiled at the image of her laughing and kissing anyone else.

"Did I lose you?" Colin asked, sounding perplexed. "You go through a tunnel or something?"

"Reception can be pretty lousy in the mall. How about I let you go, and you can text me later if your plans change or if you have a definite time for when you'll get to town Tuesday? You still have a spare key?"

"Yep."

"Travel safe," Justin said. *And slow down.* Even if his brother had days when he didn't care whether he lived or died, there were others who did. At least Colin always wore his helmet.

He disconnected the call and walked back through the mall, wondering how much closer Arden was to Santa now. Had Hope's picture already been taken? He didn't—

"Justin!"

He stopped in his tracks, scanning the bustling crowd for the pint-size owner of that now-familiar voice. Despite some mixed feelings about letting Kaylee get too close to him before moving away, he couldn't fight the smile already spreading across his face. The little girl was holding hands with a disgruntled Elisabeth; they'd been about to enter the ice cream shop.

He greeted the six-year-old with a friendly fist bump. "What brings you to the mall?"

"Ice cream!" Kaylee declared.

"I'm running some errands for my mom while Dad and Steven are snowmobiling. The ice cream was just an added bonus," Elisabeth said.

"As I recall, you used to get some wicked cravings for ice cream." He remembered her, wearing only his shirt, blending peppermint milk shakes to cool them down after a hot couple of hours in her bedroom. To Kaylee he said, "Bet I can guess what Beth's gonna order. Peppermint ice cream."

Elisabeth ducked her gaze. "Everyone orders peppermint this time of year. It's the seasonal special."

But Kaylee looked impressed with his deductive skills. "How do you know what she's gonna order?"

"Because peppermint's been her favorite since even before she was born."

Patti Donnelly had once shared the information that peppermint had been the only thing that soothed her queasy stomach when she was pregnant, so she'd taken it in as many forms as possible—peppermint tea, hard candies, peppermint ice cream. It had always been one of Elisabeth's favorite flavors, and Patti claimed her daughter's fondness for it had started in utero.

"You can't have food *before* you're born," Kaylee said, exasperated.

"You don't think babies get food in their mommies' tummies?" he asked.

"Elisabeth?" The little girl tugged on her guardian's

purse, her face very serious. "How do babies get inside mommies' tummies?"

Elisabeth smacked her forehead with the heel of her hand, then glared at Justin. "Don't you have somewhere else—anywhere else—to be?"

"Actually…" He gave her a sunny smile and lied through his teeth. "I was headed in for some ice cream myself."

As he followed them to the counter of the creamery, he texted his sister to let her know he'd be back soon but had stopped to spend a few minutes with Elisabeth and Kaylee. He included their names because he knew it would get him out of trouble for bailing on Santa duty, but as soon as he hit Send, he wished he could take it back. Arden had an overactive imagination where he and Elisabeth were concerned, and he shouldn't encourage that.

Her response text "Elisabeth, huh?" was positively dripping with I-told-you-so. She followed it up with "Take your time!!!!!!" Her use of exclamation marks was not subtle.

He groaned, drawing Elisabeth's notice. She was probably eager for any excuse to end to her whispered conversation with Kaylee about rescheduling their baby-making talk.

"Problem?"

"Sister," he said as if the two words were synonyms. "I'm sure you can relate."

"I'm guessing yours didn't ruin clothes she borrowed without asking?"

"No. She's just convinced that she knows better than me."

Elisabeth made a sympathetic noise. "I get that one a lot, too."

"I want a sister," Kaylee announced to no one in particular. "Or a baby brother. Babies are cute. Are you going to have a baby, Elisabeth?"

"Not anytime soon," she evaded. "It's our turn next. Why don't we concentrate on what you want to order?"

"The all-you-can-mix!"

One of the most popular features of the creamery was the massive selection of fruits, candies and other goodies they would hand-blend into your ice cream on a slab while you watched.

Kaylee proudly delivered her order to the teenager behind the counter. "Chocolate ice cream with butterscotch candies, watermelon licorice, pineapple chunks and Goldfish crackers."

Justin's stomach clenched at the unappetizing combination. "This is why you're one of my favorite kids on the planet," he praised Kaylee as they watched her ice cream being prepared. "It takes a lot of bravery to try new things. Some people are too afraid to step outside their comfort zone." He ordered a cookies-and-cream shake for himself and a caramel swirl to take to Arden.

Kaylee scrunched her nose. "What's a comfort zone?"

"I'll explain it on the way home," Elisabeth offered. "We should get our ice cream to go. Dinner's waiting for us in the slow-cooker, and Steven will probably get to the loft before we do."

Since they were all three going in the same direction, Justin continued his conversation with his young friend as they walked. "Did you see Santa while you were here today? That's where I'm headed."

"*You're* gonna sit in Santa's lap?" Kaylee asked incredulously.

"No, I'm here with my sister and Hope."

"But the baby can't even talk yet. How can she tell him what she wants for Christmas?"

"Good question."

"Oh, she's full of good questions," Elisabeth said wryly. "Keeps me on my toes."

He bit back a laugh, imagining how interesting their car ride home was going to be. "Maybe if Santa spends a few minutes with Hope, he'll just know what to bring her. The nice thing about babies is, they don't need much to make them happy."

"I don't need much to make *me* happy, either," Kaylee declared, her voice full of virtue. "I only want one thing this year. To stay in Cielo Peak."

Elisabeth's expression was equal parts regret and frustration. "We talked about this. Steven's job will be in California."

"Couldn't Santa help find him one here?" Kaylee asked hopefully.

"It doesn't work that way, honey."

"Then I don't wanna visit Santa." She burst into tears. "And I *don't* want Christmas!"

Chapter Eight

On the ride home, Elisabeth tried to change Kaylee's mind about her Christmas boycott. But she gave up after a few minutes, sensing that she was only strengthening the girl's stubborn resolve. Classic case of be careful what you wish for. Hadn't she told Justin the other day that it would be a relief for Kaylee to have a normal childhood meltdown like other kindergarteners had? The day had started promisingly, and Elisabeth had hoped they'd have a nice dinner tonight before Steven left early the next morning.

There seemed like no chance of that now.

When they walked into the loft, Steven was chopping cucumbers for the bowl of salad on the kitchen island. It was already filled with romaine leaves and tomato chunks. He smiled at both of them in greeting. "How was the mall? Packed solid?"

Kaylee startled them both by shrieking, "I hate you! *You're* the reason we have to go to stupid California."

Elisabeth gasped. She'd never heard Kaylee speak to anyone like that. "You're entitled to be upset about moving, and you're even entitled to be upset with me.

But that does not mean you get to be rude. Tell Steven you're sorry."

The only answer was a mulish look.

"Kaylee, you have to apologize, or you're going straight to bed." It would be the first time Elisabeth had ever considered sending her to bed without dinner, but since the girl had recently gorged on ice cream, it wasn't as if she were in danger of wasting away during the night. Ironically, Elisabeth had offered to buy the ice cream because Kaylee had been so good today, so patient and well-behaved. Was it seeing Justin that had stirred her up, or had this outburst been inevitable even without his presence?

"You're being mean," Kaylee accused. "You hurt my feelings!"

"You hurt mine, too," Elisabeth said gently. "By acting out and not listening. Go up to your room, and we'll talk after you've calmed down." Maybe Kaylee would apologize then, and this would be behind them.

Steven moved behind her to rub her shoulders. "Tough day?"

"Only the past thirty minutes or so," she said. "Maybe she got overstimulated by the mall. Santa was there, and she asked if Santa could get you a job here. So that we don't have to move."

He sighed. "Oh, boy."

"I know I can't let her act like that, but I also know this is her first Christmas ever without her mom. Sometimes I'm not sure exactly where the line between compassion and discipline is."

"I wish I could help, but I honestly don't know what

to say. For what it's worth, I think you're doing great with her."

"Thanks." She appreciated the moral support, but... Was it naive that she'd been expecting more?

When she thought back to the emotions she'd experienced after accepting his proposal, she had to admit that one of them had been relief. She hadn't wanted to do this alone. But now she was engaged and, when it came to parenting Kaylee, she felt just as alone as ever. After a few minutes, she went upstairs to see if she could reason with Kaylee. The girl had cried herself to sleep and was curled up in the middle of the bed, her soft breathing punctuated with the occasional weepy hiccup.

She came back downstairs feeling deflated. When Steven had arrived in town, she'd assured herself that this would be the perfect time for the three of them to become even closer, to start preparing for life as a family. So why did she feel as if they hadn't made any progress?

The two adults ate a subdued dinner, both of them seeming lost in their own thoughts. As they cleared the table, he said, "I'm close to a breakthrough, I think. I just need to nail it down." He absently kissed her cheek, then returned to his laptop.

It was funny—she'd once told her sister that she and Steven used their time more efficiently than most couples because of their long-distance status. Yet, under the same roof, she felt as if they'd barely spent any time together at all. She idly flipped through TV channels, hardly registering the pictures that passed as she mulled over her relationship with Steven. He'd often complimented her as the most understanding girlfriend he'd ever had, but it was easy to be understanding about someone's work habits from a whole state away.

Just as, she imagined, it was much simpler to be supportive of someone's child-rearing difficulties when you didn't have to live with the child in question. She knew from her own experience how challenging instant parenthood was. Did—

"Mommy! No!" The childish screams were full of pain and fear, slicing right through Elisabeth. She shot off the sofa, bolting to Kaylee's side. She cradled the little girl against her, feeling her rapid heartbeat and her hot tears against her neck.

By the time she'd soothed Kaylee back to sleep and had her tucked under her blankets, Elisabeth's hands were shaking. *Michelle, what am I doing? Help me out here.* Elisabeth had read one school of thought that said not going to a child's side would eventually teach the kid to calm down on their own and become more self-sufficient. The opposing viewpoint—that if she proved to Kaylee she didn't have to face life's traumas alone the girl would start to feel more secure and the nightmares would lessen—made far more sense to Elisabeth. Besides, she had plenty of memories of her own mother stroking her hair and murmuring assurances after bad dreams.

Steven was waiting for her at the bottom of the stairs, his gaze pinched with worry. "That sounded worse than usual."

She nodded. "We need to talk."

"I was afraid of that," he said ruefully. "I've been horrible, haven't I? Glued to my laptop. What if I can promise you that things will get easier after this version is released?"

She laughed without malice. "And what about the next version? And the one after that? You haven't been horrible at all. You've always been a wonderful friend, Steven."

He winced.

She sat on a step, feeling too drained to go farther. "I adore many things about you, but if I'm being honest, I think I looked at you as a life preserver. When I suddenly lost a friend and became a mother, I felt like I was drowning and desperately needed help."

"Which I'm not successfully providing."

"That's not the problem." At least, not completely. "You deserve a woman who loves you for you, not one who loves you because you represent salvation from single-parenthood. It was so comforting to feel like I'm not alone, but that emotional security blanket isn't enough to uproot Kaylee. She's not ready for this, and neither am I. Between you and me? With all the demands of relocating and the learning curve on your promotion, I'm not sure you are, either."

He sighed. "You're a hell of a woman, Elisabeth Donnelly. I'm going to miss you."

"You can still call me," she offered, "whenever you need to talk."

"Maybe not. Maybe it's time we stop being each other's crutch and see where life takes us." He smirked. "And now that you're free to act on any attraction to a certain ex-boyfriend, I wouldn't want to interrupt."

"What? Justin? No!" She jerked her thumb upward, indicating the bedroom above them. "I have that little girl to think of. Justin Cade couldn't handle the emotional responsibility of caring for one person, much less two."

His expression remained skeptical, but he didn't argue. "I hope you find the right guy someday, for you *and* Kaylee." He lifted her hand and brushed a kiss across her knuckles. "I'm just sorry I couldn't be him."

MONDAY WAS, AS PATTI always put it, "Christmas Eve Eve." Yet Elisabeth felt anything but jolly when she strode into work, a red-eyed Kaylee in tow. A steaming mug of coffee sat on the edge of her dad's desk, but he wasn't in the office. It was just as well since neither Elisabeth nor her daughter was fit company right now.

Kaylee had been up twice more during the night, and neither of them had gotten enough sleep. This morning, Kaylee had thrown a fit over breakfast, changing her mind three times about what she wanted to eat until Elisabeth decreed she no longer had a choice. Today had been when Steven was originally scheduled to leave, so they'd said goodbye to him as planned. Kaylee had been so sullen with him that Elisabeth had decided immediately she couldn't tell the girl about the broken engagement or canceled move. What if Kaylee thought, even subconsciously, that she'd been successful in running him off with her bad behavior? Elisabeth couldn't encourage her to use tantrums as a means to get her way. The other, less likely but equally troublesome possibility was that Kaylee might guiltily blame herself for Steven's departure.

No, it was definitely best to wait before broaching the subject with Kaylee.

Elisabeth supposed she could tell the adults in her life about Steven, but sharing the news of yet another failed relationship was the last thing she wanted to do at Christmastime. While this breakup hadn't left her quite as emotionally shattered as the split with Justin months ago, she was angry with herself. How had she let something with no future get so far? Elisabeth had always valued her family and respected their opinions, so why had she been so stubborn about this? *Hell, even Justin freaking Cade could see it wasn't going to work out.* Then again, that shouldn't count. Not working out was his default mode.

Two days before Christmas, she'd given back a diamond ring she never should have accepted in the first place and had to figure out how best to deal with Kaylee whenever she switched into hellion mode. Was the behavior an aberration, brought out by extreme stress, or did it signal the beginning of a new, prolonged phase? In which case, there wasn't enough aspirin in the world.

Elisabeth booted up her computer, hoping for a few minutes of calm before anything pressing demanded her attention.

But Kaylee stood up from where she was supposed to be coloring on the floor and announced defiantly, "I'm going to see Chef Bates."

"Oh, no, you're not. Chef Bates loves you, but he's got his hands full with the breakfast crowd right now. If you show me you can behave—"

"I don't want to live with you anymore! I want to live with Justin."

"Well, that's not an option," Elisabeth retorted.

"Am I interrupting something?" Lina asked as she strolled into the room. Kaylee dashed over to embrace her aunt.

Lina returned the hug. "Morning, sunshine."

Sunshine? Not in this room. They were more like a couple of solar eclipses this morning, completely blotted out by the moon.

"Everything okay?" Lina asked. "Are we just feeling down because Steven had to leave, or—"

"I'm *glad* he's gone!"

"Kaylee Truitt, that is enough." Elisabeth knew the girl had been through a lot, but she wasn't raising her daughter to be a disrespectful brat.

Lina's eyes widened at the hostility in the room. "Kaylee, why don't you go out to the reception desk? My mom's got breakfast pastries there. I need to talk to Elisabeth alone, okay?"

"I hope she doesn't hurt your feelings like she hurt mine," Kaylee said as she flounced out.

They watched her walk to the desk that was within view of the office, then Elisabeth plopped down at her own desk, head in her hands. "I've had her less than six months, and I've ruined her. Maybe I wasn't cut out to be a parent."

"Don't beat yourself up. Mom and Dad raised you, so you know they must have been doing something right, but you also saw what I was like. My wild moments don't mean they were doing a bad job. Parenting's always been tough. Consider this your initiation into the club."

"Thanks. I just… People's childhoods shape who they are." She thought of Justin, of all he'd suffered in his younger years and his resulting inability to let people close. "I'm afraid that what I do and say could affect her whole life."

"Lots of things will affect her, but you can't control all of them. Hell, you can't control *most* of them."

Elisabeth arched an eyebrow. "Well, that's terrifying. Thanks."

"Don't mention it. It seems as if the two of you could use some space. Want me to take her off your hands for a while?" Lina offered.

Although Elisabeth wouldn't come in to work on Christmas Eve or Christmas, that had still left today, when she had to contend with Kaylee being out of school. She hadn't meant for it to inconvenience her family. "The mood she's in, I'm not sure I want to inflict her on you."

"I'll bet getting her fingernails painted and a partial pedicure would cheer her up."

"Probably, but that sounds too close to rewarding bad behavior. If she gets her act together this morning, she can join you for some beauty treatments after lunch."

"See, that was an example of responsible parenting," Lina said. "You balance sternness and caring. Stop doubting yourself."

She managed a half smile. "You mean show a little self-confidence? Too bad I'm not more like you."

"More like *me*? Bite your tongue. I'm a mess. If you don't believe me, I have the phone numbers of some ex-boyfriends, former high school teachers and credit card companies you can call."

"Thanks for the pep talk. You may not be perfect, but you're a good sister."

Lina winked. "And don't you forget it."

THE CIELO PEAK patrollers covered four resorts, including the Donnelly lodge, and a number of backcountry and Nordic trails. Because the past two nights had dumped so much snow and conditions were expecting to worsen by afternoon, Monday was nonstop action. Whatever seasonal melancholy Justin had been experiencing lately was chased away by other demands. He had no time to think about his brother's arrival tomorrow or Elisabeth's engagement.

It was the way he preferred to live—in the moment, the bracing cold rough against his face where his skin wasn't completely covered in protective gear. He chatted with guests on the mountain and encouraged as many as possible to check out a beacon from the top shack and take the free hour of training. No one ever thought they'd need a beacon, until they did. Several skiers and snowboarders expressed frustration at the predicted weather later today that would close even more trails. Patrollers had already roped off two that morning.

He'd just made it back to the base station when a call came over the radio that Graham Donnelly had reported two missing teenagers.

THERE WAS NOTHING like a mountain to give a person perspective. Elisabeth had been completely stressed out when she'd arrived at the lodge, but a six-year-old with a bad temper was not a life-or-death situation.

Accidents—and, occasionally, even fatalities—happened in ski communities, but overall, the Donnelly lodge had been lucky. This was their first real crisis of the season.

Adrenaline was coursing through Elisabeth's body, but she worked to keep her tone as calm as possible while speaking to Amanda Lamb.

Twenty minutes ago, the middle-aged Mrs. Lamb had shown up in a panic at the registration desk. She'd been hysterical, so it had taken both Patti and Elisabeth to piece together the story. The Lamb family, including sixteen-year-old Meredith, were staying at the lodge. Meredith had befriended a cute nineteen-year-old guy who was visiting along with some college buddies.

"She's obviously got a crush on him, but he's too old for her," Amanda had sobbed. "I told her to stay away from him, and she was furious with me, said that all I ever do is try to ruin her fun."

When the time came for the Lamb family to hit the slopes that morning, Meredith had complained of cramps and asked to stay in the room and read. Her parents had agreed. But after a couple of runs, when the chairlift was put on a wind-hold, the Lambs had decided to return to the lodge for lunch and to check on Meredith.

"She wasn't in the room," Amanda said, sounding horrified anew by the discovery. "But her phone was there. She never goes anywhere without it! I thought she must be at the vending machine or the gift shop. Something quick."

As the Lambs grew progressively worried, Mr. Lamb had tracked down one of the college boys, who admitted Meredith had secretly met with his friend. Both teens had last been seen leaving the lodge, but the boys had expected their friend back by now because they had plans that afternoon. The Lambs were frantic.

And quasi-murderous. It had taken both Javier and Elisabeth's dad to pull Mr. Lamb away from the college kid. "That's my daughter out there!" the man had been yelling in full view of other diners. "If anything happens to her..."

Graham Donnelly took the father to a patrol station, and Lina joined Meredith's younger siblings in the restaurant. Elisabeth ushered the weeping Mrs. Lamb into her office to give her a place to wait where her tears wouldn't alarm her other children. Kaylee had been coloring in the corner, but Patti challenged her to a few rounds of air hockey in the game room, diplomatically removing her from the office.

"Th-that was your l-little girl?" Amanda asked, blowing her nose. She'd already gone through an entire box of tissues, so Elisabeth pulled out another from the supply closet.

"Yes." She didn't see the point in explaining that Kaylee wasn't hers biologically. *She's mine in all the ways that matter.*

"Daughters will break your heart. Every damn day, they'll break your heart," Amanda said. "But you love them more than anything in the world anyway. Meredith isn't a bad kid, overall. Honors student, careful driver, sweet to her little brothers. But, still... Some days, it seems like everything I do is wrong and that she completely hates me."

"Know that feeling," Elisabeth commiserated. When the phone at her elbow rang, both women jumped.

"Oh, God," Amanda wailed. "Have they found her?" The question she didn't ask was, in what condition had her daughter been found?

The caller was Elisabeth's dad. "Patrollers have Meredith," he said. "She's going to be fine."

Elisabeth relayed this news to Amanda, who began crying even harder.

"Meredith and the boy she was with ducked under ropes onto a closed trail," Graham continued, explaining their mysterious whereabouts.

Elisabeth's heart sank. Those trails were closed for a reason. People didn't understand, looking at the snow-capped trees and seemingly peaceful white landscape, how deadly conditions could be with no warning at all.

Her father confirmed her fears. "He was buried, and she couldn't find him. She went running for help. Justin Cade was one of the patrollers already looking for her, and he's bringing her to the station. Tell Mrs. Lamb that she's not hurt, only scared. A rescue team's out looking for the boy."

Elisabeth thanked her dad for the update and hung up, vastly relieved that she had good news for Amanda Lamb but still worried for the other missing teen. Who they now knew was missing under an avalanche of snow. Her pulse pounded. She'd seen avalanches in person, and the comparison that always came to mind was lava—an unyielding spill crashing down the mountain, a threat to every single thing in its path.

"It's okay. Meredith is okay." She squeezed Mrs. Lamb's hand, surprised to find her own eyes were damp. "Your daughter was lucky. She was found by one of the best patrollers in Cielo Peak, my friend Justin."

"Is Justin here?" a high-pitched voice demanded.

Elisabeth looked past Amanda to Kaylee. "What are you doing back here? I thought you were playing with Grandma."

"Lina has to give someone a back rub, so Grandma and I are going to have lunch with those kids. I wanted my crayons. Where's Justin?"

"Out doing his job." Elisabeth angled her chin, gesturing toward the window and the snowy expanse beyond. "He saved this woman's daughter."

Kaylee didn't seem as impressed as Elisabeth expected. Or maybe she just assumed that her hero was constantly saving people and therefore wasn't surprised by the news. "Can I go see him?"

"No, you take your crayons and get back to Grandma. I'll be watching you cross the lobby to the restaurant, so no detours," she warned.

Kaylee glared. "I want to see Justin!"

"Maybe later. He's busy right now. Adults have responsibilities. And so do children," she added. "Your responsibility is to do what you're told."

Glaring, Kaylee snatched up her crayons and stomped out of the room.

Amanda gave a watery laugh. "Guess it's not just sixteen-year-olds who throw fits when you try to keep them from the men they admire. But my kid disobeyed me for a smug nineteen-year-old who doesn't think the rules apply to him, whereas your daughter seems smitten with a bona fide hero. At least she has discerning taste."

Chapter Nine

People who paid money to visit ski lodges sometimes felt cheated when they didn't actually get to ski—even though their hosts couldn't do a thing to control weather conditions. Elisabeth was exceedingly grateful for the guests who were in good spirits and even the ones who were disappointed but understood the logic of not skiing in a snowstorm. Why didn't more people exhibit common sense? And why call it "common" if so many lacked it?

As Monday afternoon wore on, and it became clear skiing was probably going to be impossible for the rest of the day, she found herself dealing with an increasing number of grumbling guests. Some seemed to be getting stir-crazy even though they'd only been stuck in the lodge for a few hours. She had to step in when a woman in the gift shop became verbally abusive with the cashier.

As Elisabeth crossed the lobby to return to her office, someone tapped her on the shoulder. Another complainant? She smoothed her features into a calm, accommodating expression, even as she fantasized about that move in kung-fu films, where a small protagonist was able to grab the hand of the burly cretin behind her and flip him to the ground.

She spun around. "How may I— Oh." Seeing Justin in his red patrol coat, his eyes brighter than ever in a face abraded by the elements, was like drinking hot chocolate. Liquid heat coursed through her body, sweet and addictive. "Hi."

"Hey." His blue-green eyes crinkled at the corners as he smiled down at her. "Thought I'd stop by and ask how Meredith's doing."

"Better, thanks to you. She could've been seriously injured."

"She could've been killed," he corrected somberly. "That boy was in bad shape when we found him."

She shivered at the thought of the kid's narrow escape. "Dad drove down to the hospital to check on him. The doctors say no long-term damage was done."

"He or either of those other two frat yahoos have any family in the area?" Justin asked.

"Not local, but his mom and stepdad are about an hour and a half away. I called them earlier."

No doubt the vitriol the boy's stepfather had spewed at her stemmed from a sense of helplessness and fear, but that hadn't made it any more pleasant to endure. It flabbergasted her that the man had threatened to sue instead of praising the rescue efforts of those who'd saved his son's life after he chose to ignore the posted warnings and sneak into an area he knew was off-limits. To say nothing of his taking a minor with him, thereby putting her in harm's way.

She met Justin's gaze. "I am so sick of people yelling at me today."

"That bad, huh?"

"Worse." She squeezed her eyes briefly shut, as if she could ward off her headache through sheer force of will. "Even Kaylee got in on the action. By the way, she doesn't want to live with me anymore. She informed me she wants to move in with you. To tell you the truth, if her attitude doesn't improve, I may let her."

He looked genuinely distraught by this news. "I am so sorry. You warned me at the tree place that this was supposed to be a time for her and Steven to do some father-daughter bonding. I didn't mean to get in the way of that. Running into you at the mall was an accident, but I guess it wasn't very sensitive of me to offer babysitting on Saturday."

She was touched by the contrition in his voice. "Amanda Lamb told me today that drama between mothers and daughters is normal and that I should expect plenty more of these blowups over the next decade. So I guess from that perspective, I'm doing something right," she said wanly.

Justin cupped the side of her neck, idly rubbing a knot of tension with his thumb. "You're doing a ton right," he said, continuing the massage in slow, deep circles. She fought the urge to press into his touch and purr. Before, he'd worked here during the summer season as a hiking guide and first-aid administrator. If he ever wanted to come back, he should talk to Lina about hiring him to give massages. Women would be lined up around the mountain.

"Do you want me to say hi to Kaylee while I'm here," he asked, "or would it make your life easier if I left quietly, without encouraging her?"

"She had a rough night last night with no decent sleep and everyone around here's been pretty frazzled today. A quick hello from you may help turn the tide. I think she's upstairs with Lina getting her nails painted right now, though."

He pointed to some vending machines outside the game room. "Lina's over there getting a soda."

"Oh, then Kaylee's probably back in the office." Elisabeth led him behind the reception desk and into the office. Which was empty. She poked her head out of the room and called to her sister across the lobby.

"What's up?" Lina asked.

"Is Kaylee still getting her nails done?" Elisabeth asked.

Her sister frowned. "No. I haven't seen her since lunch."

"What? I dialed your extension for her earlier, right before I had to deal with an accusation against house-keeping." A man had said his was wallet was stolen, but it turned out that his wife had simply moved it. "I told Kaylee she could ask if you were ready for her and if not, she could keep coloring. When I got back to the office, she wasn't there, so I assumed…"

No one could enter the office without going behind the enclosed reception counter and the lodge was full of Kaylee's extended and honorary family, so Elisabeth had felt safe leaving the little girl alone for a minute. Now she battled gruesome images of worst-case situations.

"Breathe," Justin reminded her softly as if he felt her rising panic. "We'll find her."

Elisabeth wanted to believe him, but knew she

wouldn't feel calm again until she could see Kaylee with her own two eyes. "She didn't talk to you?" she asked Lina.

"We talked. She asked me about coming up like you instructed, but since no one can ski right now, our appointment book filled right up. I couldn't squeeze her in yet."

So first Elisabeth had disappointed her by telling her she couldn't see Justin, then Lina had reneged on the mani-pedi offer? Elisabeth tried to put herself in Kaylee's shoes, thinking like a miffed kindergartener. "Maybe she slipped into the kitchen to visit Chef Bates." The little girl would've wanted a sympathetic ear and some comfort food.

Lina nodded. "She worships him."

Elisabeth lifted the receiver from the phone on her dad's desk and punched the button for the restaurant. "Javier, have you seen Kaylee over there? Would you mind checking with the chef?" He put her on hold and as she waited, her palms grew clammy.

She was probably overreacting because of the day's earlier events—too much leftover adrenaline in her system looking for an outlet. Just because there was some superstitious saying about bad things happening in threes didn't mean there was any truth to it.

Breaking up with Steven, those kids on the closed trail, Kaylee…

"Ella no está aquí." Javier's accent was thick with apprehension. "I am sorry, Senorita. The chef, he has not seen her since lunchtime."

Her fingers shook. "Thanks, Javier. I'm going to look around the first floor. If you see her, buzz my cell phone?" The back of her throat burned. So did her eyes. She raced toward the doorway. "Kaylee? Kaylee!"

A few guests stopped what they were doing and glanced in her direction, but no Kaylee emerged from the game room or sat up from one of the comfy sofas in the lobby. Meanwhile, Lina rang the salon upstairs to see if Kaylee had decided to plead her case in person. "Maybe she was on the elevator going up at the same time I was taking the stairs down. For that matter, have we checked the elevators? You know she loves punching the buttons."

But no one had seen her on the third floor. Lina checked in the women's restroom, and Justin talked to some guests exiting the elevator banks.

Lina's voice was beginning to quiver. "Should we check with Javier again?"

"He knows to call me the second he sees her," Elisabeth pointed out.

"Right." Lina nodded, her eyes unfocused. "I just really expected that she'd be with Chef. He's her favorite person on the planet next to you."

Oh, God. "No. No, he isn't—at least not for the past few days," Elisabeth said, hoping against hope that she was wrong. She recalled Kaylee's tearful declaration that she wanted to go live with Justin and the girl's excitement when she'd thought he was here earlier.

Justin flinched, his eyes darkening with realization. "It's me, isn't it? I'm the person you think she went to see."

"She was asking for you." Elisabeth stared in horror out the window, where wind was whipping the snow against the glass. "And I told her you were out there."

"You shouldn't be here." Justin didn't know why he wasted his breath on the words. They were nothing he hadn't already said a dozen times. When he'd tried to warn Elisabeth about the biting winds and rapidly diminishing visibility, it had only redoubled her determination.

"That is my daughter out there," she'd told him. "You can go without me, but you can't stop me from looking for her on my own, so what's it gonna be?"

As Justin and Elisabeth set out, he'd radioed Trey Grainger to see if he could bring a couple of more guys to help sweep the area surrounding the lodge. Back at the lodge, Lina and Patti were turning the place inside out in case Kaylee was holed up in some corner playing cards with one of the guests' kids. Justin prayed she was. Part of the area surrounding the lodge was road, and visibility was already lethally low. The odds of a driver seeing a small child and being able to stop quickly in icy conditions—

He flashed back to the day he'd learned his sister-in-law and young nephew had been killed. Justin was trained for rescue. He should be cool and detached out here, his actions dictated by hours of training and experience. Instead, he felt almost paralyzed with fear.

Stop thinking about the car accident. Don't think about the roads. On the positive side, not many people would brave driving in these conditions. On the negative? It was getting dark. His gut clenched as he imagine a six-year-old runaway with no gloves or flashlight out in this blizzard. Even *he* felt frozen through, and this was the office where he reported for work every day.

He squinted through the fading light, studying a distant structure. "Remind me—what's that cabin? Would it be unlocked?" If he were a scared kid out in the freezing cold, possibly too turned around to retrace the path to the lodge, wouldn't the logical course of action be seeking any convenient shelter?

"When my grandparents first opened the lodge, that was where they lived." Elisabeth led the way. "We rent it out to families who are willing to pay extra for separate bedrooms and their own kitchen facilities, sometimes we use it for special events, but it's empty right now. It should be locked, though. I have a key, but Kaylee wouldn't be—" She sucked in her voice, then swore with feeling. "*Damn it.* Justin? I dropped the key ring."

He knelt beside her, both of them digging with their gloved hands. At first, they were too intent on their task to hear the muffled sound of the cell phone ringing inside her jacket.

Elisabeth yanked off one of her gloves, letting it fall heedlessly into the snow while she put Lina on speaker phone. "What is it? Did you find her? Is she okay?"

Justin's heart stopped. If anything had happened to Kaylee, happened to her because of *him*—

"You're not going to believe this." Lina's voice was a strangled combination of laughter and tears. "She was asleep the whole time. In the Cupboard of Doom."

Cupboard of what?

Elisabeth rocked back on her heels, looking dazed, as if she couldn't process the good news. "That can't be right. Small as she is, she still wouldn't fit. And we would've noticed immediately if she'd opened that door. A landslide of stuff would've cascaded out."

"I was as surprised as you. Dad called to say he's at the diner in town, waiting for the worst of the weather to pass. I told him about Kaylee disappearing from the office, and he suggested I check the cupboard. Turns out, he's been coming in late at night and slowly clearing it out. Getting it organized after all these years was going to be his Christmas present to you. She's fine. Want to talk to her?"

It had obviously been a rhetorical question since Lina wasted no time handing over the phone. Then they both heard Kaylee's small voice. "Elisabeth? I'm sorry. I didn't mean to hide and scare you and make you leave."

Thank God. Justin didn't think he'd truly accepted that the girl was okay until they heard her. When they'd left the lodge, he'd been so afraid that he'd caused this. He'd been choking on the irony—that a kid with a chance at a stable home with two parents might risk her own safety over a loser like him. Listening with half an ear to Elisabeth and Kaylee, he continued pawing through the snow until he came up with the keychain.

Holding it up for her to see, he cocked his head toward the cabin door. "How about we finish this conversation inside where it's warm?"

ELISABETH STOOD BENEATH the steamy spray of water and evaluated the situation. She was snowbound for the night in a quaint cabin with the only man who'd ever broken her heart. It had been a very unsettling day. No, it had been a horrible day, the worst in memory since Kaylee had come to live with her.

When she and Justin had stepped inside the cabin,

he'd suggested they wait out the blizzard here instead of trying to track back to the lodge in the dark. Now that they knew Kaylee was safe, it seemed unnecessarily reckless to court pneumonia or frostbite. Here, they had electricity, food, plumbing and two beds. And luxurious hooded bathrobes with a velour finish and the lodge's logo on the pocket.

Her pulse had stuttered when Justin had assessed her from head to toe and declared, "We should get out of these clothes."

For safety reasons, she'd repeated to herself over and over. Not sexual ones. They'd both been wearing quality protective gear, of course, but the kind of wet, bitter cold they'd slogged through was pervasive. Besides, she couldn't help feeling as though the clothes she'd worn all day were contaminated with fear and anguish and guilt over not paying better attention to Kaylee, or speaking to her too sharply.

Luckily, there was a laundry room here. By the time Justin and Elisabeth set out tomorrow morning, their garments would be freshly cleaned and dried.

Aware that Justin also deserved a hot shower, she turned off the water and quickly toweled off. The robe was thick and generous, completely covering her from her chin to her toes. Despite being swathed in soft fabric, being naked beneath it made her feel scandalously exposed. She ignored the irrational sensation and stepped out of the bathroom, the hem of her robe trailing on the hardwood floor.

In the main room of the cabin, cedar-scented flames now crackled in the fireplace. "I see you've made yourself useful," she said approvingly. "Shower's all yours.

While you're in there, I'll scavenge for dinner supplies."

"Sounds good. Back in a sec," he told her.

There weren't any perishables in the kitchen, but there were a number of soups available. She pulled out a selection of them and lined up some options next to the electric can opener. When she reached into a cabinet of pots and pans, the excessive metallic clanking made her realize how badly her hands were shaking. The shower had helped bring her stress level down from stratospheric heights, but there was more progress to be made.

She plugged in the portable CD player on the counter and dug through the rack next to it until she found some soothing instrumental music. Then she went to the back of the walk-in pantry, looking for the slim wine rack that hung on the wall. There weren't many bottles, but one was a start.

With a glass of cabernet in her hand and a jazzy piano solo filling the room, she started to feel a little lighter. When she hadn't known where Kaylee was, she'd felt as if she were suffocating on her own fear, unable to breathe in oxygen past the dread. What would she have done if Lina's call had been different? If Kaylee hadn't been unharmed when she was found? Tears pricked the corners of her eyes. What if… Horrible possibilities played out in her mind, each worse than the last.

"Hey! Hey, you okay?"

Elisabeth jerked her head up, wondering how long Justin had been standing there in front of her, his rugged features pinched with concern. He was a welcome focal point, a distraction from her awful thoughts. Because of his height, the matching robe he wore didn't cover quite as much of him as it did her. The material stopped around his knees, revealing his well-muscled calves and bare feet.

"This is stupid, isn't it?" She wiped furiously at her eyes, embarrassed to be caught in the middle of her meltdown. "I didn't cry when we were looking for her, so what the hell is the point in crying now?"

"Totally normal. I see it post-rescue all the time." Taking her hand, he drew her toward the couch. "You were being brave earlier, holding it together, following my instructions. But now comes the aftershocks. The release of all that pent up emotion. The relief that's too strong to contain."

They sat down, and he put his arm around her, pulling her close and letting her cry on his shoulder. He seemed big and safe and larger than life.

Slowly, the tears ebbed and details began to penetrate her senses. The fire was heating the room nicely. Balmy lassitude seeped through her bones, driving out the last of the cold, and her muscles were relaxing under Justin's touch. He'd started by patting her back in a steady, impersonal manner. It wasn't much different than how she comforted Kaylee after some of her bad dreams. But at some point the patting had turned to something gentler, more intimate. He was rubbing slow circles that traversed from the small of her back all the way up to the bare skin of her neck.

Meanwhile, the instrumental CD had progressed from meditative pieces to earthier music. Whatever song was playing now bore no resemblance to the previous innocuous track. This piece had started with a piano and violin, two solos that fused into a single haunting melody as the rhythm escalated in a beautifully relentless beat. She took a deep breath, hoping to clear her head, but the scent of Justin's skin made her dizzy.

"You smell good," she murmured.

Angling his head away slightly, he peered down at her. "Can't take credit for that." He grinned. "It's from the quality bath products your family keeps stocked here."

"No. I wasn't talking about the soap. Underneath it, you smell like...you." Warm, familiar, alluring. She wanted to nuzzle his skin. That thought caused her to sit bolt upright. What was she doing?

He raised his eyebrows at her abrupt departure. "Everything all right?"

"F-fine." Except that every cell in her body seemed to have just realized it had been over five months since she'd had sex and felt that was too long. She had no business snuggling up to her ex and commenting on how good he smelled. *Although*...if she was babbling compliments, at least she'd stopped shy of telling him he had magic hands. "I left my wineglass in the kitchen. I—"

"On it," he volunteered. He stood, pivoting his body toward the kitchen. Unfortunately, he hip-checked the lamp on the end table. The light fixture crashed to the ground. "Hell. Sorry about that. I'm not usually clumsy."

"I know."

Usually, he moved with mesmerizing, fluid grace.

On the slopes, on the dance floor and in the bedroom. Not that Justin necessarily needed the convention of a bed.

He bent down to pick up pieces of the lamp, but stopped, staring blankly at the floor. His voice had a raw, hollow quality to it. "You're not the only one shaky after what happened."

That confession sliced through all her defenses. He'd been as scared as she had been. And she imagined that admitting it wasn't easy on his male pride. She scooted to the end of the couch and wrapped her arms around his shoulders in a hug. It was her turn to comfort him.

"She's okay," Elisabeth whispered, her words for both of them.

"Yeah." He touched her forehead to his, his relief palpable. "She's okay."

They stayed like that, her leaning over the arm of the couch and him kneeling in the floor, and even though Elisabeth registered on an intellectual level that this proximity was too close to be wise, she couldn't force herself to move. The CD must have reached its end, because the music had stopped. The only sounds were the snap and sizzle of wood in the fire and their breathing. Breathing that grew faster and more ragged the longer they remained in place.

If someone had asked Elisabeth later, she honestly couldn't have said which one of them leaned in for the kiss, which one moved that final inch that separated them. All she knew was that Justin's mouth was on hers, where it belonged. Need surged through her, shivering along her nerve endings and making her tremble.

He rose slowly, until he was in place to gently tip her back on the couch.

Once she was stretched across the sofa cushions, he joined her, his weight on top of her such a perfect fit that she almost whimpered at how good it felt. Earlier, when they'd been out in the blizzard, she'd felt as though she might never be warm again, but now heat pulsed in her veins. Hot, achy desire. The snow and fear were from a fading nightmare; only this was real. Only Justin.

She kissed him deeply, threading her fingers through his hair and holding him close. Meanwhile, his fingers were busy with the sash on her robe. She hadn't managed to untie his yet, but she'd pushed the fabric apart to give her better access to that chiseled chest.

"You and knotted belts," he whispered against the curve of her throat. "How do you make them so freaking sexy?"

"I do?"

"You have this trench coat dress…" With a soft growl, he nipped at her skin. Then he lifted his weight just enough that the material of her robe slipped away from her body, leaving her exposed to his hungry gaze. His expression was so intense it almost made her self-conscious, but before insecurity could take root, he lowered his head and captured the tip of her breast in his mouth. Any fleeting shyness she'd experienced was annihilated by the sharp pleasure that blasted through her.

By the time he replaced his lips with his fingers, plucking at her pebbled nipple as he kissed his way down her body, she was nearly frantic. Her body clenched with need, her thighs had fallen open in wanton invitation. She needed him inside her.

But he had other ideas. At the first brush of his tongue over her, she cried out his name. He wrung shouts and pleas from her as she writhed beneath his mouth. Thank God they were in an isolated cabin, their carnal activities drowned out by the howling wind.

"Ah, Beth, the way you feel." The rasp of his voice was a turn-on all by itself. "The way you taste…"

Her orgasm rose quickly, striking with such electric force she imagined it was like being hit by lightning. Really, really *good* lightning.

Yet somehow, even at the edge of bliss, it wasn't quite enough. She heard herself say, "I want you inside of me."

He groaned. "You're killing me, baby. There's nothing I want more, but I wasn't exactly prepared for this. Unless you've got some kind of birth control…"

"No." She'd never done well with the Pill, and since she and Steven hadn't— Mortification seized her previously limp muscles. Steven. As of yesterday morning, she'd planned to spend the rest of her life with him. Now, less than twenty-four hours after their breakup, she was being intimate with a man she'd sworn she would never be involved with again. She sat up, hugging the robe tight to her body. "What did I just do?"

Justin stared at her, his mouth twisted in a wry smile as if he couldn't decide whether he was insulted or amused. "If it makes you feel better, darlin', I think technically *I* did it."

At the thought of exactly what she'd let him do, and the equally intimate things she'd eagerly wanted to do in return, her face flamed. She tunneled her fingers in her hair, pressing her palms to her temples. "I'm so sorry," she said, ashamed of her needy behavior and the state she'd left him. "This was radically unfair to you."

"To me?" He didn't look at her. "Or your fiancé?"

"I don't have a fiancé." She held up her bare left hand. "Not anymore. We said our final goodbyes this morning."

Justin paled. "I can't say I thought he was the best thing to ever happen to you, but I hope I—"

"It wasn't your fault. Ending things before they went any further was best for everyone." She couldn't honestly say yet what she wanted. But she knew what she didn't want. "Kaylee and I aren't going to California."

And she was 100 percent positive that she'd made the right decision. It occurred to her that at no time today had she wished he was here with her. She hadn't wanted him to hold her and tell her Kaylee would be safe.

"So you're single?" he asked haltingly.

"Free as a bird. Just like you."

The silence was swollen with possibilities, all the things she or Justin could say but didn't dare.

Finally, he turned to meet her gaze. "I think we may need something stronger than red wine to drink."

Chapter Ten

"Got it!" came Elisabeth's triumphant cry from the cabin's main bedroom.

When Justin had asked about liquor, he'd been half kidding, but she'd snapped her fingers and said, "The family wall safe. I'd forgotten all about it."

While he waited for her to pillage the mysterious safe, he'd looked through the CD rack and settled on a compilation of '80s hits. He'd seen the conflicting emotions ravaging Elisabeth's face after the shortest afterglow ever, and he'd experienced his own twinges of regret. Despite his reputation for seeking out a good time wherever he could find it, he had always steered clear of other men's wives and fiancées. His parents had loved each other deeply—he himself refused to ever marry, but he still respected the institution. While he was relieved to learn she and Steven had broken up, she'd barely had a chance to process the split before Justin had unthinkingly pounced on her. He'd needed to hold her so badly he hadn't stopped to consider obstacles or consequences.

After all the anxiety and remorse today, he hoped his musical selection would help lighten the mood. It was hard to beat yourself up while you were walking on sunshine or building cities on rock and roll.

"Look what I found." She held out a nicely aged single barrel bourbon. "Emergency stash for medicinal purposes. Like how they used to put casks of liquor around the necks of Saint Bernards for mountain rescues."

He suspected the brandy barrels were a myth, but who was he to argue with a beautiful woman bearing high-end liquor?

While searching the cabinets for glass tumblers, they discovered an unopened bag of marshmallows. Under other circumstances, this evening might have been his idea of a perfect date.

Elisabeth took the marshmallows out of his hand. "Soup first, dessert later."

"Killjoy," he teased.

"I have to practice being tough now that I'm a mom."

Mom was such an odd word to ascribe to her. On the one hand, she seemed far too young and sexy to be the mother of an elementary schoolchild—Michelle Truitt had been a few years older. But he had to admit that Elisabeth had adapted well to her new role. When she'd warned him this evening that she'd be going into that snow with or without him, she'd been fiercely maternal.

As they waited for the soup to boil, he took a generous slug of bourbon, trying to suppress how shaken he'd been by Kaylee's disappearance. That's what being a father would mean—that soul deep vulnerability at all times, the fear that something precious to you could be ripped away with no warning. As his brother had experienced firsthand.

On the mountain today, Meredith Lamb had escaped generally unscathed. But Justin had seen searches go the other way. And he knew the bald terror that Mr. Lamb and other dads suffered while waiting for news.

Thankful for the calming influence of the liquor, he took another smaller sip. "So explain to me again about this Cupboard of Doom?"

"It's a storage space in the office, lower to the ground than most closets but very deep. My father, unbeknownst to anyone, has been working late to clean it out. Apparently he didn't shut the door all the way last night and when Kaylee saw the edge cracked open, she got curious. It was like discovering her own little cave. She didn't sleep worth a damn last night, so I guess it's not surprising that she drifted off."

While the adults in her life had been standing only yards away trying not to hyperventilate, she'd been snoozing away, completely oblivious.

Elisabeth stirred the soup, looking pensive. "Funny thing is, I always thought Dad needed me to organize that cupboard. He talks about needing me—they all do—like I'm the one who makes the big decisions. But I don't think they realize how much *I* need *them*. I'm not even sure I realized it myself until today. Family is…"

He stared into the bourbon, wondering how long Colin would stay in town before taking off again, how long it would be before Arden began gathering boxes and asking Justin to help her pack.

"This is what you were trying to warn me about when you asked me to lunch last week, isn't it?" she asked. "I was too stubborn to listen."

He didn't blame her. "I haven't given you much reason to value my opinions."

"But I do." Her tone held a note of wonder, as if she herself was surprised to discover how much his thoughts still mattered to her. She smiled up at him. "In everything but decorating Christmas trees. You're a complete disgrace in that area."

When he laughed, her hand moved toward him as if she'd been about to touch his face. Instead, she simply shook her head.

"Your eyes seem so out of place." Although the words might have sounded vaguely insulting, her expression was a different matter.

"Out of place? I recall a certain redhead who used to tell me all the time that she loved my eyes." He stepped closer, holding her gaze for effect.

Her cheeks flushed prettily. It was endearing that after the explicit nature of what they'd shared on the couch she still reacted to such harmless flirtation.

"It's wintry and bleak tonight," she said, pointing out the window. "Hostile. I gotta tell you, after today, I'm kind of over snow for a while. Then there's you, with those eyes like the Caribbean. Sun and seduction, the ability to make a girl feel like she's a million miles from here."

He blinked. "For a woman who cultivates such a no-nonsense, aloof image, that was damn near poetic."

"Yeah, well." Turning her back to him, she ladled hearty potato soup into bowls. He almost missed it when she mumbled, "You know me better than that. You always have."

It was a one-eighty from her position on Saturday,

when she'd claimed that she had changed and he no longer understood her. Now, she made herself vulnerable by admitting she'd been wrong, admitting that he saw the parts of her she normally hid. He was humbled. Of all the people in Cielo Peak, what had he done to deserve these private glimpses at such an amazing woman? How could he repay her trust in him?

I can't be what she needs. She had agreed to marry Steven, had actively planned to spend the rest of her life with him. Even though their relationship hadn't panned out, he was obviously the type of man she envisioned loving. And he was about as far from who Justin was as a man could get.

Then again, if Elisabeth had been satisfied with what Steven had to offer, she wouldn't have broken the engagement. As Arden had noted, Elisabeth hadn't looked truly happy with him. She'd never had that goofy, I-am-so-crazy-about-this-person smile that Arden got whenever Garrett set foot in a room.

One song on the CD faded into the next, and a low beat started, accompanied by a fiddle and then the boisterous trill of piano, leading into the vocals of "Come On, Eileen." On a whim, Justin grabbed her hand and spun her in a tight circle, whirling around to the catchy up-tempo song. When her green eyes lit with laughter, he felt as if he'd won the lottery. This was how she should look—giddy, flushed, full of life and energy.

Improvising dance moves in floppy robes was silly. There shouldn't be anything sexy about it. Yet he kept getting tantalizing glimpses of her legs, kept remembering how easy it was to tug on that sash and have her gorgeous curves bared to him. And judging from the glances she stole at him from beneath her lashes, she wasn't unaffected by their physical closeness. Was she thinking about kissing him again?

He briefly considered ransacking the cabin in search of condoms, but a latent shred of chivalry stopped him. What he and Elisabeth had shared earlier had been spontaneous combustion, nothing premeditated. He was thinking more clearly now. Clear enough to note that she'd been through a hell of a lot today. He wasn't so depraved that he went around seducing single mothers when their emotional defenses were down.

If he kept telling himself that over and over, he might make it through the night.

When the song ended, they took their soup—and the bottle of bourbon—into the living room. She sat on the sofa with her legs tucked up beneath her, the voluminous robe swallowing her whole. Setting his stuff on the end table, he glanced toward the hearth. Behind the grate, the fire had dimmed from active flames to glowing embers.

"Guess I should see what I can do to get that going again," he commented. "It's pretty dark in here."

"Yeah. You know what this room could really use?" she asked with a straight face. "A lamp."

He grinned. "Smart-ass."

An hour later, once they'd eaten their fill and dutifully washed the dishes, he asked her if it was time to revisit those marshmallows. They found fondue skewers to roast the marshmallows in the fireplace. Elisabeth's were evenly brown on all sides. His caught on fire. She mocked his charred dessert, haughty in her marshmallow superiority.

"I'll have you know, these are still gooey and delicious on the inside," he told her.

"I'll take your word for it. I prefer to be patient. With just a tiny bit of extra time and care, mine turn out perfectly every time."

"Have I told you how good you are with Kaylee?" he asked. "A natural-born mother."

She whipped her head around, startled. "Where did that come from?"

"You manage to make even roasting marshmallows a life lesson. She's gonna learn a lot from you, and you'll make sure she has fun and develops plenty of self-confidence along the way."

"Thank you." She looked so staggered that it was almost disturbing. It wasn't as if he'd never paid her compliments before.

"What's with the shock—don't you think you're doing a good job with her?"

"Now might not be the best time to ask me," she said drily, "considering you and I are stuck here because I lost her."

"Beth, that could have happened to any parent. And you didn't lose her. She was right where she was supposed to be." He shrugged. "We just weren't looking hard enough. Maybe I'll get you some of those *Where's Waldo?* books for Christmas. You know, for practice."

She reached into the bag and threw one of the untoasted marshmallows at him. "When I tell her we aren't going to California, maybe she'll lift her Christmas embargo. I'm worried about how to handle it, though."

"Christmas?"

"Telling her the wedding's off," she clarified. "I want to be compassionate about what she's been through, but that doesn't give her a full-access pass to be a brat when things don't go her way. In this particular case, it worked out that she's going to get what she wants, but I can't let her think it's because of how she behaved. Do you think she told me she didn't want Christmas just because she was ticked off about the move, or do you think, on some level, she really is dreading the holiday without Michelle?"

"I couldn't say." Justin gazed into the flames. "For me personally, Christmas hasn't been the same since my mom died. I'd prefer to skip it altogether. But Kaylee's younger than I was when I lost my mother, probably more resilient. Arden still adores Christmas. She makes a huge fuss—"

"Oh, no! Arden." Elisabeth pressed her fingers to her mouth. "I won't be able to hire her for the wedding after all. I'm a lousy friend, asking her to pencil us in on such short notice, then canceling."

"She'll understand." In fact, he doubted his sister would be the least bit surprised. It seemed she'd known what she was talking about when she'd implied Elisabeth wasn't meant to be with Steven. *But that does not mean she's right when she says Elisabeth and I belong together.*

The CD had stopped, and the fire was dying down again.

"Sorry there's no TV in the cabin," Elisabeth said. "You're probably bored out of your mind."

"Not exactly." He would welcome a distraction, though. Because he'd been watching her lick the sticky bits of marshmallow from her fingers, and he was rock hard beneath the robe.

"I think there are some games in the closet." She stood, wobbling a bit when she caught her toes in the hem of the bathrobe. He steadied her, taking the opportunity to slide his hands up her smooth calves. "Th-thanks. So, um, games."

At the end of the room was a narrow closet. She opened the door, marveling at the selection. "Jeez. We've got a ton of them."

He joined her, ostensibly studying the boxes but mostly enjoying her nearness.

"Anything in particular you're good at?" she asked.

He smirked. "You tell me."

She narrowed her eyes in a quelling look that would have been more effective if he hadn't seen the flash of heat in her gaze first. And if her earlier, throaty cries of satisfaction didn't still ring in his ears.

"To rephrase," she said sternly, "is there a particular board game you prefer?" She read off the names of a few that were meant for young children, another he'd never heard of, and Clue. "Although, I think you need three players for that one. We also have Monopoly."

Which could stretch on for hours. He didn't think he and his siblings had ever successfully completed a full game during his youth. "Beth, we're trapped here for the night, not 'til spring thaw."

Her eyes flickered with emotion. "Is that how I make you feel? Trapped?"

She clearly wasn't talking about tonight, and he hadn't been prepared for the question.

"No! No, you make me feel..." Humbled and strong

and possessive and weak. Aroused and unbalanced and bewildered. He backed away. "I know I hurt you when we broke up, probably more than I realized at the time, but you have to know I didn't leave because of anything you did wrong. I—"

"Please tell me you aren't about to insult me by re-cycling the 'it's not you, it's me' chestnut."

"Um. More bourbon?"

She pulled a box out of the closet and slammed the door.

He peered over her shoulder. "What did you de-cide on?"

"Jigsaw puzzle." She lifted her chin. "There comes a time when you shouldn't play games anymore."

YAWNING BEHIND HER HAND, Elisabeth looked up from her three-quarters completed aerial view of Paris and checked the time.

From the other side of the card table, Justin shook his head at her. "If you're tired, why not go to bed?"

Even though she was finally starting to get drowsy, she didn't think she was in the clear yet. If she went to bed too soon, with her mind still active, she'd wind up tossing and turning, plagued with thoughts of what could have happened today. She'd lie awake question-ing whether a big family Christmas would be just the thing to help Kaylee heal or if it would be an insensitive reaction to her loss. And, most of all, she doubted she'd be able to sleep because she'd be tormented by thoughts of Justin and how good his body felt against hers.

Earlier, he'd given her a climax that had made up for five long months, but he'd been left frustrated by their encounter. Should she remedy that? There'd been a moment of temptation when he spotted a pack of cards behind the napkin holder on the counter.

"I've always liked poker," he'd said. "I don't actually have any money on me, but there are other varieties we could play."

Given how few clothes they wore, it would take about two minutes for a game of strip poker to deteriorate into touching and kissing. *Yes, please.* It was an undeniably enticing proposition. But letting herself fall under Justin's spell was a dangerous path, one she'd taken before—she knew where it led and how it ended.

"It's nearly midnight," she observed, sidestepping his question about bed. "Almost Christmas Eve."

He suddenly raised his gaze to the ceiling. "I just realized what this cabin is lacking. Mistletoe!"

She rearranged a couple of pieces that went in the middle of the Eiffel Tower. "Do you really hate Christmas?"

"*Hate's* a strong word. But I was serious about being perfectly happy to skip it. My mom loved the Christmas season. She had one hundred and one ways of making it special. I remember *that,* but the specific details elude me. Like, in my mind, I can still smell this cake she baked every winter, but for the life of me I can't remember what it was called or the ingredients she used. She had this angel we put on the top of the tree, and I don't know what ever happened to it."

He rose, going to rinse out his tumbler, clearly stalling at the sink to collect his thoughts. "Kaylee lost her mother months ago. Hopefully, the distance between then and now will let her enjoy Christmas. But my mom died right in the middle of the holidays. Dad checked out emotionally, he was just a mess. And Colin was scrambling, doing the best he could. We were in pure survival mode. We weren't bothering with niceties like the good tablecloth or preserving Mom's traditions. One by one, they pretty much fell by the wayside. Does your family have any quirky Christmas traditions?"

"Pajama day," she admitted sheepishly. It was lame, but it was theirs. "It was something my mom instituted about thirteen years ago, on the first Christmas in memory when Dad left the lodge in employee hands and didn't stop by to check on things. We stayed home all day, exchanging presents, nibbling on leftovers, watching black-and-white holiday classics. It was so decadently lazy that Mom decreed we weren't even going to get dressed. Now, every year, Lina and I give her special pajamas on Christmas Eve.

"Which means my mother now owns way more pairs of Christmas pajamas than one person needs," practicality forced her to add, "but it's our goofy ritual. She loves it. Sometimes, Dad or I have to spend an hour or two at the lodge on Christmas day, but as soon as we walk in the door, we humor Mom by changing into pajamas. She has a photo album just for the annual group picture of all of us in our pj's."

Justin was smiling at her story, but it didn't hide the sorrow in his eyes. "It's not that I hate Christmas. But I spend December with this nagging feeling that I'm doing it all wrong, that I'm overlooking—that I've forgotten too many of—the little touches that made Christmas with her special. It's like, by not observing those traditions, I'm losing her all over again."

Elisabeth tried to swallow past the lump in her throat. She and Justin had been together for months, but he'd shared more about his mom in the past five minutes than he had during the entire time they'd dated. All Elisabeth had really known was that Rebecca Cade had died of cancer. It was clear Justin had been very close to her and missed her even decades later.

It was alarming to think of Kaylee and wonder how she'd feel twenty years from now, whether Elisabeth would be enough to make up for the mother she'd lost or if Kaylee, like Justin, would still have a large empty place in her heart.

"Maybe you should come up with your own traditions," she suggested tentatively. "From what you've said about your mom, she would've wanted that."

"You're probably right. But family was always at the core of Mom's customs. Arden and her cowboy are starting a family, so they'll be coming up with their own holiday practices. Colin's in the wind. I don't plan to have a family. I don't have a steady girlfriend or a dog. I don't even have a goldfish."

It stung, to see him in pain. She forced a smile. "Would you like one? A goldfish, I mean? I'll wrap up the fish, you get me those Waldo books, and we'll meet for a gift exchange. I'll bring the fruitcake."

"Cades don't do fruitcake. Our holiday dish of choice is lasagna with burned edges. It's Colin's specialty."

"What about when your mom was alive?" she prompted. She understood what he meant about some of the traditions being lost in the mists of time, but there had to be a few things he remembered clearly. "What was one of her specialties?"

"Lemon bars," he said after a moment's thought. "I've looked recipes up on the internet and experimented, but none of them were exactly right. I know it's stupid. My mother was a complex and loving woman. Her existence can't be boiled down to a lemon bar."

"It's not stupid," she protested. "You loved her." It was a revelation, seeing this depth of feeling in him. Just as she knew the people in town viewed her as Lina's quieter sister, they looked at Justin and saw a flirtatious ladies' man—someone who was fun to share a round with, someone who would have your back on the mountain, but not someone who let himself care. She felt as if she'd been entrusted with a precious secret.

"So, I've revealed to you my embarrassing lyrical tendencies about your Caribbean eyes," she said, "and now I know the importance you place on lemon bars. Should we make a pact not to tell everyone that I'm a would-be poet and you're a big softie?"

He gave her a conspiratorial smile. "Even if we did tell, who'd believe us?"

JUSTIN WAS TAKEN aback by the enthusiastic hug Patti Donnelly gave him the next morning. Hadn't she, less than a week ago, been glaring at him in the lodge restaurant and looking for any excuse to toss him out? But now, she greeted him as though he were the conquering hero come home. Next to him in the lobby of the lodge, Elisabeth was similarly being smothered. Her father had crushed her in a bear hug, while Lina hovered behind him, impatiently declaring, "Me, me, me! My turn."

Because Kaylee was short, she was able to dart between the adults, stealing underneath them to first hug Elisabeth, then throw her arms around Justin's knees.

Considering Elisabeth had spoken with her family last night on the phone, and again this morning, he thought this welcome was perhaps overkill, but so what? Life was short, and loved ones were allowed some eccentricities. Besides, he was glad to see Elisabeth and Kaylee so joyfully reunited. He hoped that when the girl was one day grown and looked back on her childhood with an adult's understanding, she could appreciate how Elisabeth had thrown herself heart and soul into parenting.

Mr. Donnelly clapped Justin on the shoulder. "Thanks for bringing her back safe, son. We're grateful you went looking for Kaylee. I feel terrible that I indirectly caused so much trouble."

"Dad," Elisabeth said, "no harm done. We spent the night in a warm, cozy cabin, not on the floor of a bat-infested cave. But I have to admit, my curiosity kept me up most of the night. You've got to show me the new and improved Cupboard of Doom!"

He laughed. "Didn't think your old man had it in him, did ya? I just wanted you to know, even though we'll miss you and you'll always have a place here as long as you want it, we'll be okay when you go to California."

"About that…" Elisabeth's gaze flew to Justin's, as if she was seeking his assistance on how to break the news. He wasn't sure what the problem was. Based on everything he'd heard, the Donnellys would be thrilled with her decision.

Then again, he knew she'd agonized over how to best tell Kaylee. He smiled at Kaylee. "Has the dining room started serving the buffet breakfast yet? I'm starving." At the little girl's nod, he asked, "Elisabeth, would you mind if I borrow Kaylee for a few minutes? I hate to eat alone."

He was stunned when Lina fell into step with him. "You probably want to stay with your sister. Spoiler alert—she has a big announcement to make."

Lina lowered her voice as Kaylee skipped ahead to pick up a plate. "You really did it, then? You got rid of him."

Was it only because of his guilty conscience that her words sounded like accusation? "I did no such thing. It's not like I ordered a mob hit. All I did was ask Elisabeth if she was sure about her decision. Turns out, she wasn't. But that has very little to do with me."

"Uh-huh." Lina crossed her arms over her chest.

He huffed out a breath. "I thought we were cool. What gives? First, you badger the hell out of me because you think the engagement is somehow my fault. Now that she's called it off, I'm still getting the stink eye."

"We *were* cool. Before you spent the night shacked up with my vulnerable sister in a romantic cottage."

Romantic? It wasn't as though there were silk sheets and a tub for two. The cabin had been sparsely furnished—even more sparsely now that he'd broken a lamp—and rustic. Then again, who needed silk sheets? All he needed to put him in a romantic mood was Elisabeth. Last night, she'd gotten to him in ways he hadn't expected, ways he'd never really experienced before. He'd walked out of that cabin feeling somehow altered.

"If I find out you're taking advantage of her…" Lina snapped her fingers. "Hey! Are you even listening to me? I'd hate to waste perfectly good threats on a guy too spaced-out to heed the warning. Don't forget, I'm the—"

"Yeah, I got it. You're the evil twin," he finished for her. She was not, however, the dangerous one.

WHEN ELISABETH TOLD her parents that Steven was out of the picture Patti Donnelly shrieked with joy. Repeatedly.

Surreptitiously glancing at the ceiling to watch for falling plaster, Elisabeth told her mom, "I'm not sure that's the appropriate parental response for when your daughter tells you she's calling off a wedding."

"In this case," Patti argued, "it is. You're staying! You'll be here with us where you belong. Steven was nice enough, but I don't think he was the great love of your life. Now you're free to follow your heart wherever it may take you." She left no doubt as to what direction she thought that should be. Elisabeth wouldn't have been surprised if Patti offered to draw her heart a map.

"I don't mean to throw you guys out—Daddy, I know this is your office, too—but can I have a few minutes alone? I need some space, some time to process everything."

"Anything you need," Graham told her.

"Remember," Elisabeth told her parents, "don't

breathe a word of this to Kaylee. I need time to tell her in my own way."

"We promise," Patti said. She waited until she'd cleared the doorway to add over her shoulder, "While he's still here, I'm going to invite Justin to have Christmas dinner with us. When you talk to him next, remind him the dress code is pajamas, won't you dear?"

"What— Mom, wait." After everything he'd confided last night, Elisabeth doubted that Christmas with her family was Justin's idea of a good time. But if there was anyone who could pressure him into it, it was Patti Donnelly.

Oh, well. Elisabeth could always call him later to assure him he wasn't obligated to attend. *On the other hand...* She herself had pointed out that he needed new Christmas memories. He'd said he didn't have anyone with whom to make those memories. Could Kaylee's hero worship help distract him from his habitual Christmas blues? Elisabeth could recruit him on the pretext that having him there would be healthy for the little girl, who would also be making some fresh holiday memories this year.

In light of Justin's experiences, Elisabeth planned to ask Kaylee about some of her traditions with Michelle. Maybe it wouldn't work to implement any of them this year, but Elisabeth would write them down, maybe start a journal for when Kaylee was older. She wouldn't let her friend be forgotten and didn't want Kaylee to grow up feeling adrift from her heritage.

Wasn't heritage as important as moving forward? She thought again of Justin's sadness at losing cherished traditions and wondered if she knew someone who might be able to help. Arden had been very young when her mother died, but talking to her was worth a shot. Elisabeth reached for the phone.

"Cade Photography," Arden answered.

"Hey, it's Elisabeth. You have a minute?"

"For you? Definitely! What's up?"

"For starters, my wedding. Which won't be taking place." Every time she told someone, the decision felt more right and the words came easier.

She and Steven had met when she was struggling to cope with Michelle's death and Steven had been at a career crossroads. They'd vented and bonded and offered each other emotional sanctuary. It had been exactly what she needed at the time. But it wasn't what she wanted for the rest of her life. Not without more to elevate it.

Michelle had been a single mother because she'd believed it was better to raise Kaylee alone than be with the wrong person. Elisabeth had a more thorough understanding of that philosophy now. Hopefully Steven's words would prove prophetic, and she *would* find the right man. If not, she had a lot of good people in her life and had been blessed with a lot of love. That would be enough for now.

Once they'd finished their postmortem of her engagement, Elisabeth changed the subject. "One more thing before I go. We need to discuss lemon bars."

Chapter Eleven

After the blizzard the night before, there was plenty of work to be done to make the mountain safe. Justin threw himself into trail maintenance and clearing hazards, keeping busy enough that he didn't think about Elisabeth. At least, not more than once every three minutes or so.

The hazards that couldn't be immediately dealt with were marked with bamboo poles and flagging. Meanwhile, Justin and Trey Grainger, his partner for the morning, were checking for important signage and snow fences that had been knocked down so they could be returned to their rightful positions and stabilized.

One sign seemed to be missing entirely, and Justin scouted the area for it. If it couldn't be found, he'd need to alert the Hill Captain. But his concentration kept getting fractured by Patti's unexpected invitation before he'd left the lodge. The Donnellys wanted him to share their Christmas dinner tomorrow? He was the guy who'd broken their daughter's heart, the guy who'd quit his job with them in the middle of a summer season filled with hikers, bird-watchers and clients who'd heard good things about Lina's spa services.

Since Elisabeth had been shut in her office, and Justin had needed to report for duty, he hadn't even been able to ask her if she wanted him there. Did *he* want to be there? With Patti Donnelly gushing over him as if he'd single-handedly saved her daughter from a death of exposure and Graham calling him son like he always had and Lina glaring daggers as if she suspected him of impure designs on her twin?

She's not wrong.

He most assuredly did not want to join the Donnellys for Christmas dinner. But he recognized that if it had been Elisabeth who'd asked him, he would have said yes. In a heartbeat.

"Yo, Cade." Grainger skied over to where Justin was, peering at him through his goggles. "Something on your mind today? You're not usually this quiet."

"Just want to fulfill our duties so you can get home to your family. It's Christmas Eve." There would still be patrollers active today and tomorrow, but the ones with seniority got to pick their shifts first. And an increased number of trail closings meant, in theory, a smaller area that needed to be supervised. "Hey, Grainger, your family have any...I don't know, special holiday traditions?"

"Like what, leaving cookies out for Santa?"

Justin shrugged. "Or something more specific to your relatives."

"My aunt Vera always has two martinis on Christmas Eve, then passes out while my wife reads *The Night Before Christmas* to all the kids. And my nephew insists on serenading my mother every year with 'Grandma Got Ran Over By a Reindeer.' He seems to think it keeps getting funnier. Is that the kind of stuff you meant?"

"Yeah, sure. Thanks for sharing."

Truthfully, Justin didn't know what he'd meant. All he knew was that something was missing. When he was younger, he'd thought it was his parents. And God knew he still missed them. But maybe it was more than that. Then again, why should he feel that way? It wasn't as if he were jealous of Grainger's gin-soaked relatives and the annual singing of annoying carols. If that was a typical family holiday, then he wasn't missing much.

But telling himself that did nothing to ease the hollow ache in his chest.

When Justin pulled up in front of his house, Colin's motorcycle was already parked in the driveway. For a second, he recalled bygone eras when he'd sought his brother's advice on girls. Would Colin have anything useful to say about the fact that Justin couldn't stop thinking about his ex-girlfriend? He didn't dare talk to Arden about it. She'd be too busy telling him "I told you so" to really hear what he had to say.

Decades ago, it had been Colin who explained the birds and the bees to Justin. The week after Justin's twenty-first birthday, he'd been telling his brother about a wild night with a cocktail waitress and had laughed when Colin had needed clarification of a term. Justin had finished his explanation with a smug "and the student becomes the master." While Justin wasn't necessarily ashamed of his past sexploits, he remembered them distantly, as if they'd happened to a buddy, not to the person he was now. That cocktail waitress had been beautiful and accommodating, but if she were to show up on his doorstep today asking for a repeat performance, he wasn't sure he could muster the enthusiasm.

Because she's not the right woman.

Hell. When had his conscience started sounding like his sister? Arden's lectures about love were annoying enough in person. The last thing he needed was her greatest hits soundtrack playing in his head.

An unexpected grin tugged at his lips. Maybe his sister being a pain in the butt about his love life was their little tradition.

He swung open the door beneath the carport and found his brother standing in the kitchen, filling a glass of water. Justin wasn't braced for the wave of relief that swamped him. He hadn't realized how truly worried he'd been about his big brother until he was able to clap eyes on him, safe and sound and in person. But this Colin bore minimal resemblance to the formerly clean-shaven veterinarian who used to carry his son Danny on his wide shoulders.

Colin had always been tall, but his frame had been proportional. The weight he'd lost made him look longer, giving the impression that he towered over Justin even though there was only about an inch difference between their heights. His dark hair had grown shaggy and wild, and the beginnings of a beard stubbled his lean jaw. Only the piercing blue-green eyes beneath his bangs were the same.

"Damn, bro." Justin stepped forward to give him a brief one-armed hug. "I see you finally gave up that pesky personal grooming that was keeping you off the cover of *Axe Murderer Monthly.*"

Colin shoved him. "Well, we don't all have your vast supply of hair products and tanning spray."

"Tanning spray?" Not bloody likely. Justin made a rude noise. "I oughta kick your ass for that."

"Give it your best shot. Should make for an entertaining three minutes before I flatten you."

"See, this is why you need to visit more," Justin said approvingly. "Arden thinks sibling relationships are all about sharing feelings and telling each other how much we care."

Colin shuddered.

"You have any lunch yet?" Justin went to the refrigerator, pulling out a soda and a container of deli-sliced roast beef.

"No, just got in. I could eat."

They'd be having a big formal dinner at Arden's that night, so they didn't need anything fancy to tide them over. Justin's plan was sandwiches and chips. But that plan went south when he realized he hadn't bought any new chips since Kaylee had snacked on the last of them Saturday—and the only bread he had was beginning to show little green dots of mold.

"Grab your coat," he told Colin. "We're eating out."

Before his brother could respond, Justin's cell phone chimed. Probably Arden wanting to make sure Colin had arrived safely. Elisabeth's number flashing across the screen was a welcome surprise.

He was grinning as he answered. "Miss me already?"

"Yes, that's exactly why I called. Pining for you has

sapped my will to live," she intoned. "I can't eat, I can't sleep, I can't update my Facebook status."

"Wow, you're in worse shape than I expected. Maybe I should take your mom up on that invitation to make sure you don't waste away."

There was a pause before she spoke again, her voice serious this time. "That's actually why I was calling. I don't want you to feel… Do you think… Isn't Arden expecting you to spend Christmas with her?"

Justin leaned against the counter. "We're having dinner there tonight. I'm going over for a few hours tomorrow, too, but she knows I have a patrol shift in the morning. And she'll have a really full house tomorrow night. Garrett's parents are coming in to be part of the baby's first Christmas, and she's invited Hugh and Darcy Connor over, too. I don't think she's really expecting me to stay for that."

He knew Arden would be more than happy for him to have Christmas dinner with Elisabeth. His sister would probably turn freaking cartwheels. But what about Elisabeth? Did the idea of his joining the Donnellys make *her* happy?

She seemed undecided. "Kaylee would be thrilled if you could make it. My folks, too. And something about you seems to stick in my sister's craw, which is fun to watch. But Kaylee's already so crazy about you…"

What about Kaylee's mother? It was a question he couldn't voice. Because, deep down, he wasn't sure what answer he wanted to hear.

"I have a radical idea," he said. "You sit through a meal with my family tonight, and I'll join yours tomorrow. Like…like a suicide pact, but with holiday dinners."

Colin snorted.

"We have to work on your holiday cheer," Elisabeth said, sounding as though she were trying not to laugh. "You honestly want me to come with you to Arden's?"

He was as surprised by the impulsive invitation as she was. But given his options, it was an unquestionably logical choice. He could spend the evening with a sappy engaged couple who hadn't seen each other in over a week and would spend the night mooning over one another, plus Colin—who tended to retreat into stony silence at these festive gatherings. Or he could enjoy the company of a woman who made him feel ridiculously good just by calling him and taking verbal swings at his ego.

A dinner spent listening to Arden's unsolicited advice about who he should date, or actually bringing a date? No contest.

"Can you get your mom or Lina to babysit Kaylee for the evening?"

"Done. Mom already invited Kaylee over to make gingerbread houses tonight and have a sleepover so that Santa can stay home and tackle these damn 'some assembly required' toys without fear of being interrupted. I think Santa can justify a dinner break. The North Pole has labor laws, right?"

"Pick you up at six," he told her, trying to pretend he wasn't already counting the hours between then and now. "See you soon, Beth."

Colin barely waited until he'd disconnected the call before asking, "Beth, as in Elisabeth?"

Justin nodded. "She and Arden are friends. I thought it would be nice if she joined us tonight. The more, the merrier, right?"

"I know I've been out of the loop, but didn't you dump her? Or is this a different Elisabeth?"

"Same one. You ready to go?"

They stepped outside, but Colin didn't drop the subject.

"You're dating her again? I've never known you to circle back to the same woman twice," he said as he opened the SUV's passenger side door. "What happened, did you run out of new ones?"

That characterization stung. Justin had always enjoyed female company, but he wasn't some pathological womanizer. Turning the key in the ignition, he informed his brother, "We aren't dating."

"Uh-huh." Colin's thick skepticism was annoying as hell.

But that was okay—Justin had the perfect idea on how to exact revenge. Many stores would be open until five today. "By the way, we're gonna need to hit the mall while we're out."

"AM I OVERDRESSED?"

Justin knew that it wasn't a rhetorical question, and he intended to answer it. He was simply having trouble finding his voice. Finally, he managed, "Wow." Although Elisabeth's clothes weren't formal, she completely outclassed his jeans and zip-necked ski sweater.

Smiling in acknowledgment of the compliment, she turned toward the rack in her foyer and grabbed a sleek charcoal trench coat. He stood immobile, appreciating the view. The black pencil skirt hugged her butt in a way that should be illegal—though he was fervently grateful it wasn't. Her black boots were sexy as hell and her silky, long-sleeved red top made him rethink his position that wearing red at Christmastime was a cliché. The color made her hair an even richer shade and brought out a wicked gleam in her eyes. The V-neck collar was going to distract him all evening.

Staring at her was definitely a better plan than listening to Arden and her cowboy exchange endearments.

"Red is your color," he said.

She paused in the act of fluffing her hair to make sure none of it was caught in her jacket collar. "Thanks, I'm glad you think so. Can you grab that gift bag by the door?" she asked, reaching around the corner for her purse. "I got a bottle of wine for your sister. Figured it was only polite to bring a hostess gift."

"What about for the guy who invited you to the shindig in the first place?" he teased. "Does he get a gift?"

"I'll be seeing you on Christmas Day, so you'll just have to wait." She shot him a sassy smile as she double-checked her front door to make sure it was securely locked. "Patience and life lessons, remember?"

Wasn't there some life lesson that championed instant gratification?

On the way to Arden's place, she told him about the Christmas toys she needed to put together tonight and how Kaylee, though she seemed somewhat subdued regarding the holiday in general, was looking forward to making her first gingerbread house. "And she's *very* excited to see you tomorrow," Arden said.

"When I told her you're going to be joining us, I got a bona fide earsplitting squeal."

"And how did she react to the other big news?"

"About not moving to California? She was as thrilled as expected. I had a long talk with her this afternoon about how this doesn't mean she'll necessarily live in Cielo Peak for the rest of her life. I have to evaluate opportunities as they come, and there may be a day when moving somewhere else makes the most sense for us. My job is to make the decisions, and her job is to communicate her opinions to me as respectfully as possible and trust me to do what's best."

All of the sudden, she sucked in her breath.

Justin laughed at her reaction to Arden's house. "Sorry, forgot to warn you about Arden's yard. Did you bring sunglasses?"

"That's just, that's… If you needed lights for your little tree, I don't know why you resorted to bats. You could have lifted a dozen strands from here, and she never would have missed them." She paused, wide-eyed, simply taking in the spectacle before her. "How are they not shorting out the entire block?"

"For all I know, her cowboy bought her a special power generator." He turned off the car. "You haven't met Garrett yet, have you?"

"No, but Arden makes him sound wonderful."

When Justin had first learned his sister was accidentally pregnant with a near-stranger's baby, he'd wanted to find the SOB and throttle him. But not even Justin was immune to the emotion between Arden and Garrett. Once the cowboy learned more about her past and forgave her for initially keeping the pregnancy a secret,

Garret had fallen for her hard. And Arden had never been as happy as she was when she was with her fiancé.

The front door flew open, and Arden rushed out in a long knit tunic and a pair of leggings. "Elisabeth! I am so glad you're joining us. It's nice to have another girl in the crowd. Colin got here just a few minutes ago, and Garrett's offered to mix up a batch of his grandfather's killer eggnog for anyone brave enough to try it. You both look wonderful. Such a cute couple!" She fixed Justin with a pointed stare. "Who could have predicted you guys would look so good together, I wonder?"

She wasn't even going to let him through the front door before starting up with this?

He sighed. "Of course we look good. She's an incredibly attractive woman, and I'm…me. We'd have to work hard *not* to look good together."

Next to him Elisabeth guffawed.

Arden rolled her eyes. "I don't know why I invite you over."

"Because your favorite pastime is meddling in my life and you get more fulfillment out of haranguing me when I'm actually around to hear it," he suggested helpfully.

"I brought you some wine," Elisabeth said, holding up the gift bag.

"Thanks. If I'm going to have to put up with him all night, I'll probably need it." Arden stuck her tongue out at Justin.

He laughed. "Good to see motherhood hasn't aged you before your time."

They all went inside, but Justin paused when Elisabeth tapped him on the shoulder.

"You know how everyone calls me the quiet, well-behaved Donnelly?" she whispered.

"That's one interpretation."

"I've decided there's no such thing as the quiet, well-behaved Cade."

He flashed an unrepentant grin. "My mama was always telling me to be good. She just never stipulated at what."

When Elisabeth got her first look at Colin through the arched entryway to the kitchen, her step faltered. "Whoa," she said under her breath. "Your brother is... different."

"I know. All that hair, he's like the Wolfman version of my brother. I hope he's in town long enough for Arden to put some weight on him." He studied Elisabeth's face. "Wait a second. You're not saying you find this look attractive?"

She hunched her shoulders in a very small, very rueful shrug. "What can I say? Some men make scruffy work," she whispered. "He doesn't look anything like I remember, and it caught me off guard. Have you had much of a chance to talk to him? Do you think he's doing better than when he left town?"

"*Better* is a relative term. When it first happened, I didn't think he would survive the week. But he manages to wake up every morning so I guess he's 'better.' It's been more than a year, though, and I'd bet his first thought each day is still wondering why the hell he's here while Natalie and Danny are gone. I suspect it's something he'll carry with him for the rest of his life, like our dad did. Granted, the rest of Dad's life wasn't long."

She stared, making him realize just how morbid his words were.

He cringed. "Sorry. I did warn you that jolly Christmas spirit isn't in my wheelhouse." But simple fun was. He'd long been known for his ability to show a lady a good time, and he was determined to tamp down this Yuletide gloom and make Elisabeth glad she was here with him.

She cupped the side of his face. "Your family's been through so much."

The sentiment, too close to pity, was discomfiting. He shrugged her words away, distancing himself from the loss. "Colin more than me." Because Colin had taken the risk, gambled on joy. And paid the price.

For Justin, dating was like skiing. It was an exhilarating rush, but only the foolhardy participated without taking precautions to protect themselves.

Chapter Twelve

Determined to be a charming companion, Justin joined the rest of his family in the kitchen where he reacquainted Elisabeth and Colin, who gave a polite nod but said nothing, and introduced her to Garrett, who grinned from ear to ear.

"So you're Elisabeth Donnelly. I'm glad we finally have a chance to meet. I've heard a lot about you," he said, exchanging knowing glances with Arden.

My baby sister has a big mouth.

"Something smells good in here," Elisabeth said.

"What's for dinner, lasagna?" Justin guessed. Thank heavens his sister made a better one than Colin ever had. "Roast?"

"Greek food," Arden said.

"Like…okay, I give up." The only Greek food with which he was familiar was gyro sandwiches. Since he couldn't recall his sister ever having eaten or cooked Greek food before, it seemed a somewhat random choice. Did Garrett have Greek ancestors in his family line somewhere?

"The main course is lamb," Arden said. "Which is what smells so good. We're also having stuffed grape leaves with a cucumber-yogurt dipping sauce and *spanakorizo,* which is a vegetarian side dish. There's baklava for dessert, and if you're already hungry there are pita chips and hummus on the table. *Opa!*"

Justin didn't know what to make of the evening so far. Garrett wouldn't stop smirking at him, Colin had barely said two words to anyone and Arden was all of a sudden throwing My Big Fat Greek Dinner Party. His only normal relative was Hope, who slept in a portable mesh crib between Arden's sofa and the kitchen entryway.

Arden stirred the vegetable dish he'd never be able to pronounce, then set the spoon on the counter. "Gentlemen, if you'll excuse me, I want to show Elisabeth the nursery."

"She's pretty," Garrett said when the women were out of the room. "Elisabeth, I mean. Arden always said the two of you should get back together—"

"Someone should tell my sister that butting into other people's lives is not an attractive quality."

"Oh, I don't know," Garrett said. "I find it fairly adorable when she's giving you hell. No point in being mad at her just because she was right about you and Elisabeth dating again."

"We're not dating."

Colin grunted. "He told me the same thing this afternoon. Sounded just as ridiculous then."

"We're friends who've known each other a long time." Friends who had made out last night. And, with any luck, would again soon. He'd been dying to kiss her since she'd opened her apartment door and smiled up at him.

A few minutes later, Arden returned to the kitchen, but she was alone.

Heaven only knew what his sister was up to. "What did you do with my da—with Elisabeth?"

"She'll be back in a second," Arden said airily. "Now, why don't you and Colin set the table for me since Garrett is changing the baby?"

But her request turned out to be a classic case of misdirection. Colin carried silverware to the table but when Justin tried to follow with a stack of plates, Arden discreetly kicked him on the ankle.

"Ouch," he grumbled. "Damn it, woman, these are your plates. I don't want to hear any complaints if you make me drop them."

Her voice was an urgent hiss. "Spill. You spent all afternoon with our brother. Did he tell you where he's been, where he plans to head next? How long he'll be here?"

"Working on ranches, working on more ranches, and no." He paused, staring at their brother in the next room. "Women don't really think scruffy is attractive, do they?"

She frowned. "What are you talking about? Stay on topic. Do you think we can convince him to give up the rambling and come home?"

"No. Look, I worry about him, too. When he's not here, I miss that sunny, winning personality," he drawled, eliciting a giggle from his sister.

"That was mean," she objected.

"Hey, you laughed. My point is, I know how you feel, but I don't think our feelings matter. He has to deal with his own issues. And if he's not ready to stick around, we can't try to force the situation. He'll just leave again."

"Am I interrupting?"

Justin turned to find Elisabeth, her eyes wide and her posture hesitant. "On the contrary, I was about to go looking for you. Arden says dinner's ready."

The meal was more pleasant than Justin had expected and not just because Arden's first culinary attempt at lamb had turned out so well. Since Garrett and Elisabeth had never met before, they exchanged lots of stories about what it was like to live on a ranch and Elisabeth's favorite—and least favorite—parts of running the lodge. Good food often had a way of making people mellow, and the wine didn't hurt, either. Even Colin contributed to the conversation, the corner of his mouth lifting once or twice in what might have passed for a half smile.

When discussion turned to Arden and Garrett's wedding, Justin's shoulders involuntarily tensed. As recently as yesterday, Elisabeth had been looking forward to her own wedding. Would the broken engagement be a sore subject for her? But when he slanted a sidelong glance in her direction, he saw that she didn't seem in the least bit agitated. She was leaning back in her chair, her finger idly tracing the rim of her empty wineglass, a serene smile on her face. She looked completely relaxed, more at ease than he'd seen her in days.

Catching him at his scrutiny, she scooted closer, her voice low. "Everything all right?"

He took the opportunity to drop his arm around her and pull her against his side. "Now it is."

She nestled against him without protest, and moments later was stroking his arm in the same lazy caress she'd used on the wineglass. But Justin was made of flesh and blood, and she was driving him crazy, calling his nerve endings to attention. Her touch was so whisper-soft that it only stoked his desire for more potent contact. Following the conversation became more difficult, but he hoped his distraction wasn't too blatant. He doubted she had any idea how maddening the feathery strokes were, how much he wanted her.

"Elisabeth, it was sweet of you to join us after putting in a full day at the lodge," Arden said. "You must be getting tired."

"Now that you mention it, I do have an early morning ahead of me." Her hand slid away from his arm as she shifted in her chair. Moving so subtly that he didn't notice at first, she lowered her hand to his knee, tracing that same idle pattern up his quad. "Maybe it's time to think about going to bed." She punctuated her sentence by gently squeezing his thigh.

Okay, he'd been wrong. She knew *exactly* what she was doing. It was only then that he noticed the grin she was trying to hide. Vixen. An answering grin tugged at his lips. He was so going to make her pay for this.

"Before we go, though," Elisabeth said, "would you mind giving me your recipe for the cucumber dip, Arden? It was fantastic."

Justin didn't think much about the women leaving the table together—he didn't currently have enough blood in his brain to do much thinking at all. But there seemed to be an awful lot of conspiratorial whispering in the kitchen for the simple exchange of a yogurt-based recipe. Wondering if he was imagining the suspicious behavior, he shot Colin a questioning look. His brother shrugged in an unmistakable *I have no idea what she's up to* gesture.

Finally, they were exchanging their goodbyes. Arden walked Elisabeth and Justin to the front door. "Elisabeth, it was lovely to see you again. Call me anytime. I've still got a few weeks before I move, and I'd love to hang out. And Justin, I'll see you tomorrow." She wrapped her arms around him in a bear hug that probably looked like an affectionate move to the untrained eye.

A bystander would have no way of knowing that Arden whispered, "I *told* you she's the one for you, you stubborn ass."

Justin didn't say anything as he took Elisabeth's hand and led her down the sidewalk through the Yard of a Million Lights. He opened her door for her, letting his hand trail down her spine. It took all his willpower not to go any lower, not to trace the beguiling curve of her butt.

As he started the car, he asked, "Enjoy yourself tonight?"

"Mmm-hmm." It wasn't dark enough to mask the laughing mischief in her gaze.

"I had fun, too. But not as much as I'm about to." He parked at the end of the street, away from his family's prying eyes, and reached for her with all the eagerness of a sixteen-year-old on his first car date.

She let out a small squeak of surprise that was absorbed by their kiss. He traced the seam of her lips, then slid his tongue into her mouth. She tasted like the honey and cinnamon from the baklava.

"Justin?" She was kissing her way up the side of his neck to his ear, and he gripped the steering wheel hard, lust roaring through him. "You realize we don't have to do this in the SUV. I have an incredibly comfortable bed back at my place."

Last night, snowed in at the cabin, he'd told himself he shouldn't sleep with her because she'd been through too much and hadn't had the chance to recover from breaking her engagement. But tonight, all that had changed. Tonight, she was *his*.

They made it to her loft in record time. But as she was unlocking the door, he stopped her with a hand over hers.

"You're sure about this?" he asked raggedly. Once they crossed that threshold, he didn't plan on there being much discussion.

She lowered the zipper on his sweater, dipping her tongue into the indention at his collarbone. "I told you last night I wanted you inside of me. That hasn't changed. Make love to me, Justin."

He fumbled for the doorknob behind her, then scooped her into his arms, kicking the door closed. He carried her to the bedroom, and had just lowered her to her feet when she insisted, "Wait!"

His muscles tensed in dread. "You changed your mind?"

"What? Lord, no." She dotted his face with reassuring kisses. "I just wanted to ask if you could give me a minute. I have sort of a present for you."

His pulse thudded in anticipation. This was the same woman who had given him those creatively naughty coupons for his birthday. He could hardly wait. "One minute," he agreed. "Sixty seconds and not a single second more."

She shooed him out of the room. He took the opportunity to pull off his shoes and socks. He'd just reached for his belt when she called breathlessly, "Okay, you can come in."

She sat at the foot of the bed. "I know this isn't your favorite time of the year, and I wanted to see if there was anything we could do to change that."

His mouth went dry. "This is a good start."

She grinned. "You did say you liked red on me." A cute Santa hat was perched crookedly on her head, and she wore a sheer red robe belted around her waist. His fingers already itched to untie it. Beneath the robe was red lace. Was it wrong that he was already having fantasies about making love to her in nothing but the hat?

It only took him three purposeful strides to reach her. He caught her by the knotted sash and drew her to her feet. "You're beautiful." He nipped her bottom lip.

Her robe didn't last long. It hit the floor as they kissed, along with his sweater and pants. Her jaunty Santa hat got knocked off somewhere along the line, maybe when she was tracing the outline of his erection with her soft hands and he gripped her shoulders. Or when she made him gasp by outlining the shell of his ear with her tongue.

When they were down to his black boxer briefs and her lacy scrap of a nightgown, he lowered her to the mattress. He slid one of her arms up over her head, then moved the other to join it. Holding both of her wrists with one hand, he swept his gaze down her body in a slow, appreciative perusal. She was the sexiest woman in Cielo Peak, but he hated the idea of any other man discovering it.

Her breasts were pushed upward by both the position of her arms and the lacy cups of the nightgown. He couldn't get enough of touching them. She was so responsive, her husky murmurs and sharp cries addictive. He trailed the side of his hand over the swell of her breast, letting his thumb just barely graze the tip. She arched her back, encouraging him to do it again.

The red lace stopped right past the feminine flare of her hips, and he could tell she was bare underneath. One tug and she'd be nude, his for the taking. After the erotic torture of touching her last night, he was ready to thrust into her, but planned to take his time. With his free hand wrapped in her hair, he tilted her head to the side, giving himself unimpeded access.

He found the sensitive slope where her neck met her shoulder and bit gently. "Have I ever told you, you give the *best* gifts?"

"It gets better," she promised. "Especially if you'd let go of my hands."

He clucked his tongue at her in a tut-tut sound. "Patience. Remember?"

She groaned. "You haven't shown a drop of patience since the day I met you, and you want to start *now?*"

"Oh, yeah." Sliding the lace cups down, he circled the peak of her breast with his finger, moving with excruciating gentleness. When her breathing grew heavier and her hips were squirming beneath him, he suckled one breast, then the other.

"Justin."

He let go of her wrists, and she plowed her fingers

through his hair, holding him close. Then he raised his head and they were kissing with abandon, their skin feverish and their limbs tangled. Needing to know she was as ready and eager as he was, he slid his hand between her legs. She was slick and tight, moving against his fingers in a way that blanked out coherent thought. He was operating on sheer primal instinct. *Need. Beth. Now.*

Lacing his fingers with hers on either side of her head, he kissed her deeply, then drew his hips back and rocked forward, surging into her. *God, I've missed you so much.* He might have said it out loud but she was kissing him hungrily, her muscles squeezing him as he slid farther inside her. White-hot pleasure jolted through him. It had been months since they'd been together, but he knew her rhythm, knew when to speed up and take her to the edge. And knew just how to send her over.

She called his name, her body contracting around him in silky spasms, and he drove into her one last time, finding his own oblivion.

Most Cielo Peak citizens didn't run their ceiling fans in December, but it was damn hot in Elisabeth's bedroom. More specifically, the man in her bed was damn hot. They'd shared a large glass of ice water and had been cuddling for the past twenty minutes, yet her heartbeat still hadn't returned to normal. Sex that phenomenal could only be described as an out-of-body experience.

While she rested her head on his chest, Justin lightly

dragged his fingers through her hair. "That was... unexpected."

Did he mean how powerful it had been between them, or that she'd had sex with him at all? It had been at the forefront of her mind since that mind-blowing orgasm he'd given her in the cabin. She'd fibbed a little at Arden's about needing to assemble Christmas presents after dinner. She'd rushed through those this afternoon before he picked her up. Just in case.

She turned her head, propping herself up on her elbow so she could meet his eyes. "I wanted you," she said simply.

"Back at you." It was gratifying how dazed he looked. She'd made a definite impact. "But, at the risk of seeming ungrateful, I don't understand what changed."

"My expectations." Could she explain this in such a way that didn't make it sound as if she was devaluing herself? "When we dated before, I thought I loved you, thought I knew what our future should look like. But the more you've opened up to me the past few days, the more I realize I never fully knew you. And as for the future...everyone talked about whether moving to California would be good for Kaylee after the upheaval in her life, but my life got turned upside down, too. If ever there was a time to consider just living in the moment, it's now. I need time to adjust to the present before I get too hung up on the future."

"So that's what this is?" he asked cautiously. "Living in the moment?"

She thought of Michelle, of his parents and his nephew. "We know better than most how life can be cut short. I overheard you and Arden talking about your brother. You said he had to deal with his issues and that nobody could force him before he was ready. The same is true of you. You mask it with your jokes and your charm and your devilishly distracting kisses, but you have a lot of baggage. I don't know when—or if—you'll ever sort through it and be ready for a real commitment. But in the meantime, for right now, I just want to be with you. That okay?"

"That," he said as he sat up to capture her lips, "is perfect. You're too good to be true."

"Good, huh?" She rolled over so that she could straddle him, smiling down into his handsome face. "Shows what you know. I'm pretty sure I'm on the naughty list."

DESPITE JUSTIN'S HABITUAL aversion to Christmas, it was impossible to dislike any day that began by waking to a gloriously naked redhead wrapped around him.

"Morning," she said drowsily.

"Merry Christmas." He pressed a kiss to her temple. "Your alarm went off."

She wiggled her hips, scooting back against him. "I heard it. I just don't want to go. Nowhere else in the world is going to be as comfortable as in bed with you."

"So we'll just have to make plans to do this again soon," he reasoned. Very soon. "But for now, I have trails to patrol and you have a little girl who will be awake soon, anxious to know if Santa visited."

He sat on the edge of the bed, his feet on the floor. "Know what else you have to look forward to? Me. I'll see you this evening."

"Don't forget your pajamas," Elisabeth reminded him, amusement threading her voice. "House rules."

Justin reached down, snagging the red lace on the tip of his finger and held it up. "If you're looking for suggestions on what pj's *you* should wear…"

She swung a pillow at his head, but missed by a mile. "You'd better go," she advised, "before I have my morning coffee and try that again."

IT WAS A beautiful, chilly Christmas morning—the kind that reminded Justin why he'd wanted to pursue a career that paid very little and carried high risks. He was in such a good mood that he didn't even mind the teasing of other guys.

"This is getting scary," Trey Grainger told Nate Washington in the hut where they all checked in each morning. "Yesterday at this time, he was barely speaking, and now he's whistling Christmas carols! It's like pod people have landed on the mountain."

Nate identified the source of Justin's good mood pretty quickly. "So who was she?" he asked as he pulled on his gloves. "The brunette from the bar last week?"

Refusing to answer any questions, Justin kept whistling all the way up the chairlift.

His family members, however, were more persistent. Once the distraction of opening gifts for baby Hope had passed, Arden kept commenting on how happy Justin looked and badgering him about whether it could have anything to do with a certain redheaded lodge manager.

He attempted to change the subject by playing on Arden's guilt. He crossed the living room and stared mournfully out the snow-crusted window, injecting as much wounded severity into his tone as possible. "Did you ever consider that I'm simply happy because I'm enjoying one of the few days I have left surrounded by my family? Colin will be headed out of town by New Year's, and you're neck-deep in wedding plans. Neither of you seems to give much thought to me here, alone and left behind, with—"

"You know, if you'd toned that down a little," Arden said, "I might have bought it. Now, tell me what happened when you took Elisabeth home! Did you kiss her? Did she kiss you? Who, when, where?"

Even though he truthfully would miss his siblings once they were both gone from Cielo Peak, it was a relief to escape his sister's interrogation and head for the Donnellys' home around three. Kaylee flung open the door while he was still making his way up the driveway. She was wearing bright yellow flannel pajamas and a pair of purple snow boots.

"Justin! Come see what Santa bought me! And come see the gingerbread houses I made with Grammy Patti. The roof fell in on my house and probably squashed anyone who lived inside, but Grammy says that's okay, it still tastes good. Boy, you walk slow!"

"Maybe that's because I'm hauling this giant sack of presents," he pointed out.

Elisabeth appeared behind the girl. She wore a pale henley shirt and a pair of endearingly ludicrous pants. They were fuzzy and printed with bright pink penguins and sleepy purple polar bears. He was feeling a little understated in his soft black top and red-and-black plaid pajama bottoms. Maybe next year, he—

He stopped so suddenly, he almost slid on the walkway and launched the packages into the air. Next year? Where the hell had that come from? What had happened to Elisabeth's brilliant plan of living in the moment?

Luckily, Elisabeth hadn't noticed his near-stumble because she was busy quietly conferencing with her daughter. Then she looked up, addressing Justin, "You'll have to excuse her. Someone ate too much of the chocolate that was in her stocking, and she's a little wired. But someone also knows that if she can't simmer down and mind her manners, she's headed upstairs for a long time-out."

Kaylee heaved a long-suffering sigh. "*I'm* the 'someone,'" she informed Justin in a stage whisper.

Grinning, he tousled her hair. "Yeah, I got that, kiddo. Can you do me a big favor? Don't get sent to time-out. It would ruin my holiday if I didn't get to spend it hanging out with you."

She beamed at him. "I'll be on my bestest behavior, pinkie swear!"

Elisabeth ushered him inside, taking his jacket from him as he shifted the packages he held. "Mom and Dad and Lina are gathered in the family room. We were watching old *I Love Lucy* episodes and talking about busting out charades or some kind of drawing game. Tell me you're good at drawing? You could be like my secret weapon."

"I can't even do a recognizable smiley face," he admitted.

"Well that's settled—you're on Lina's team."

Even though he'd never been in the Donnelly home

at the holidays before, he'd once predicted that they went all out for Christmas. He'd been right.

It was different than the spectacle at his sister's house, where everything was twinkly and automated and new from the box. Patti Donnelly's living room boasted a mishmash of handmade decorations, like a white pillow upon which someone had cross-stitched *Peace on Earth* in blue and green, and antiques, like an expensive looking snow globe from a bygone era. Blankets and pillows were strewn about the room. This was clearly not a house where Christmas was greeted with formality. He was guessing that the small beanbag with the Kaylee-shaped dent in it was where Elisabeth's daughter had been sitting. The Donnellys presided over their family from a pair of matching recliners.

Patti Donnelly popped out of her chair to come give him one of her customary hugs. Mr. Donnelly took the more relaxed approach of simply waving. "Welcome, son."

Justin presented them with the basket of gourmet meats and cheeses he'd picked up yesterday. "Merry Christmas." He turned to where Lina was sitting on a love seat, cocooned in a fleecy green blanket. "I have something for you, too, troublemaker."

She hitched an eyebrow at the square box he handed her. "I don't hear any ticking. That's a good sign." She tore through the snowflake dotted tissue paper and laughed at the sweatshirt that spilled out of the package. Then she held it up for her family to read the wording across the front: I AM THE EVIL TWIN. "Well-played, slick."

He sat down on one of the leather ottomans in the

room, and Kaylee came to his side, inspecting the two large boxes wrapped in SpongeBob SquarePants paper.

"Is one of those for me?" she demanded.

Elisabeth delicately cleared her throat. "Manners."

Kaylee wrung her hands, looking uncertain. "Is, uh, one of those for me *please?*"

He pushed the bigger of the two toward her. "This gift is, for lack of a better explanation, unfinished. There may be some accessories you need to get before you can use it."

Kaylee frowned. "Aunt Lina told me her super high heels are accessories. I can't wear those. Elisabeth says I'd break both my legs." Suddenly she straightened and faced Lina. "I just remembered. Do you know Justin calls you my 'crazy aunt Lina'?" The girl giggled. "That's funny."

Lina looked less amused. "You should hear some of the things I call him. Now, open your box already! I'm dying of curiosity."

When Kaylee saw the snowboard, she was almost beside herself with excitement. "Can we go use it now?" she begged.

"Probably not right now, and definitely not without a helmet," Justin said. "But we can go shopping for one soon, and I can start teaching you. I taught my sister, Arden, when she was about your age."

He'd never wanted to have kids, but now it occurred to him that, if he didn't, he wouldn't be teaching sons and daughters, wouldn't be passing on his skills or knowledge. *So what? You have a beautiful niece, and one day when she's old enough, you can take Hope out on the slopes.* Nephews and nieces would be plenty to keep him fulfilled.

He slid the other box across the floor toward Elisabeth. "And this is for you."

As soon as she got the wrapping paper off and saw the picture of the desk lamp on the box, her shoulders began to shake with laughter.

"I, uh, have it on good authority that you can use a new lamp, on account of some clod breaking yours."

She grinned. "I know just where I'll be putting it."

From across the room, Patti Donnelly lifted the glasses she wore on a slim chain around her neck. "Did you say that's a lamp, dear? From here it looks...kind of like a dismembered leg."

Lina was laughing now, too. "It's the lamp from *A Christmas Story.*"

"Well, a miniature replica," Justin said. "Not the full-scale one."

"The bigger one wouldn't fit on an end table," Elisabeth said, her eyes twinkling.

Kaylee had come over to investigate the lamp shade atop a woman's stocking-clad leg. "Hey! This lamp is wearing a high heel. Man, *everyone* gets to wear fancy shoes but me."

Elisabeth stepped over the little girl to hug Justin. He took the opportunity to hold her close, wondering if it would be inappropriate to kiss her in front of her whole family. *Probably.*

"Thank you," she murmured near his ear. "I love it. That movie may be completely goofy, but it cracks me up anyway."

"Now it's my turn!" Kaylee declared.

"Did you want a hug, too?" Justin asked.

"In a minute." Then she went racing out of the room, leaving the grownups perplexed.

"Mom," Elisabeth said, "do you have any idea what she's talking about?"

"Almost never," Patti smiled. "But I love her anyway."

Then Kaylee came back into the room, holding what looked like a wad of trash. "I wrapped it with some magazine pages, like how we made our Christmas ornaments," she told Justin proudly. She held it out to him. "This is for you."

"I like the crinkle method you used to keep it all together," he said, unfurling the edges. "Really saves on tape." Inside the balled up paper was more paper, this one a lined sheet from a spiral notebook.

He smoothed it out and looked at the picture. There was a tall stick figure man in a red coat and skis, with black hair that stood straight up, a stick figure woman with orange hair, green eyes and a big smile on her face, and between the two of them, a much smaller stick figure with crazy brown curls that took up a quarter of the page. They were drawn inside a big heart, holding hands beneath a bright blue sky and a smiling yellow sun. Justin found himself blinking rapidly so he wouldn't do something as unmanly as shed a tear.

"Kaylee, I… Thank you. This is perfect. I'll hang it up at my house."

"On your fridge-er-rator," she said. Stumbling over the pronunciation didn't detract from the authority in her tone. "I used to make pictures for Mommy, and that's where she always put them. I wish she could be here."

Justin locked gazes with Elisabeth, who had frozen like a startled rabbit not sure which way to flee. As far as he knew, it was rare for Kaylee to bring up her mother. He was no expert, but it seemed like a good sign that she was willing to talk about her so openly, with no prompting from others.

"I think Mommy would like the funny lamp," Kaylee continued. "And she could watch me when I learn how to snowboard. I'm going to be very good at it."

Justin reached out to pull her into a hug. He suddenly needed one. "I'm sure you will be."

"Do you think she can see me from heaven?" Kaylee asked.

"Yeah, I do." And he hoped that somewhere up there Rebecca Cade and Michelle Truitt were smiling down on their children on this Christmas morning.

"Good." With that apparently settled to her satisfaction, Kaylee straightened. "Are we going to play that drawing game now? I can help both teams. I'm very good at it."

Outside the kitchen window, silvery moonlight bathed the snow-covered yard. Elisabeth sagged against the wall with a contented sigh. It had been a wonderful Christmas. One of the best of her life. The games had been fun, dinner had been yummy and the people most important to her had shared it with her. She'd even felt as if Michelle was with them in spirit.

She wished it didn't have to end, but after an active night of little to no sleep and the early morning trip across town to her parents' house, she was tired. Kaylee was clearly exhausted. She'd crawled into Justin's lap so he could read her a funny story about a pig who wanted to fly, and her eyes were closed by the end of the first page. It wasn't like her to miss out on Justin's funny voices.

"What are you doing in here?" Lina asked. Her sudden presence might have made Elisabeth jump, if she'd had the energy.

"Psyching myself up to give one last gift," she said. What had seemed like a poignant idea yesterday, as she and Arden dug through a box that had belonged to Rebecca Cade, now seemed like a huge gamble. Arden had assured her repeatedly that it was a fantastic idea, but then, Arden was madly in love with the man she was about to marry and their beautiful daughter. She was high on life. And she wasn't exactly subtle in her attempts to nudge Elisabeth and Justin closer.

Elisabeth had tasted one of her lemon bars so she knew that they'd turned out well, but had they turned out *right?* She had no basis for comparison, and Arden had admitted she didn't even remember her mother making them. Would the tart sticky bars be what Justin recalled from childhood, the memory that would make him feel closer to his mother? Or would it just seem presumptuous that Elisabeth had tried to duplicate something so personal?

Lina came and stood next to her. "You ever wonder why Mom and Dad chose such butt-ugly wallpaper in here?" It was a distorted pattern of alternating fruits—misshapen pears and striped watermelon and hairy brown kiwis.

"I try not to think about it."

"I mean, Mom and Dad are smart people. They had no problem decorating the lodge beautifully, so you'd think their home would show the same good taste but I guess we all make mistakes. Last week, you said Justin was a mistake. Do you still believe that?"

"No." The answer was instantaneous. "I don't know yet what he is—or what he'll allow himself to evolve into—but he isn't a mistake. He's a good man who has been hurt badly."

"He is a decent guy," Lina agreed. "Much better than I used to think. Watching him with Kaylee today, and with you…either I misjudged him before, or he's matured a lot since the two of you dated. You say he's been hurt, but you're the one who had to pay for it last time. How is that fair? I don't want you to go through that again."

"I'm being smarter this time," Elisabeth vowed. "When I fell in love with him, I had stars in my eyes. I thought he was The One, and I scared him away. Now we're just living in the moment. I can't get disappointed if I don't have expectations, right?"

"Living in the moment?" Lina echoed disbelievingly. "That sounds like the kind of dumb thing I'd say if I didn't want to admit my actions have consequences or I wasn't ready to face the future. The thing about the future is, it's coming whether you're ready for it or not."

But Elisabeth *wasn't* ready to think about the future. Imagining one without Justin in it was too damn depressing, yet trying to picture him in her long-term future didn't seem fully realistic. "Go away, Leen. It was a lot more peaceful in here when it was just me and the butt-ugly wallpaper."

Lina squeezed her hand. "Maybe I'm worrying for nothing. He really does seem like he's changed. And what do I know about guys, anyway? Did you notice any blue-eyed hunks bringing *me* kitschy lamps today?"

Pep talk over, Elisabeth decided it was time to be bold. She retrieved the plate of lemon bars and returned to the living room. Her mother was working a crossword, and her dad was snoozing in his chair. But at least he was sleeping in a more dignified position than Kaylee. The little girl lay across Justin's lap with limbs flung in all directions.

"She's out like a light. Guess the picture book I chose wasn't enough of a page-turner," Justin said. When Kaylee let out a rumbly snore, he nodded. "Yep, that was pretty much my reaction to Literature class in high school. *Rhyme of the Ancient Whosits* and *Tess of the Whatchamacallit?* Bleaah."

"You should've tried reading more Shakespeare," she said. "Some great insults in Shakespeare. And some pretty good dirty jokes, too."

He laughed. "I didn't know you straight-A valedictorian types appreciated dirty jokes."

"I'm exceptionally well-rounded," she lied. High school had been a difficult time for her, particularly since it had always seemed so easy for Lina. "If I had one regret, though, right now it's that I never took Home Ec as an elective." She held the plate out. "I made these. For you."

He sat forward as much as Kaylee's outstretched

body allowed, glancing at the plate. "Lemon bars? Thanks, Beth. That's a really sweet gesture." He bit into one. "You've really—" He stopped, his eyes fluttering closed as he took another appreciative bite. "This is them, these are it. I mean…how did you do that?"

Elisabeth's heart was so full she was giddy. *I did it.* Her goal had been that look of happiness on Justin's face.

He'd had a Christmas that didn't suck. They'd awakened in each other's arms, he'd experienced new, kooky traditions like Pajama Day and she'd found a way to give him back one he'd thought lost. Too happy to stand still, she rocked back and forth on the balls of her feet.

"Arden has a box of stuff that used to belong to your mom. Mostly girl stuff, like an old jewelry box and a diary. When I explained what I wanted, she helped me look through everything until we found something promising. This recipe's got a couple of ingredients you don't normally see in lemon bar recipes. Applesauce, for one."

Justin's eyes shone with admiration. Maybe something deeper. "You are a genius. If we were somewhere without an audience right now…"

Heat spiraled through her. "Back at you," she mouthed. If they were alone right now, she could prove to herself that last night had been every bit as good as she remembered, that it had been real and not some erotic dream. But reality and fatigue were beginning to crowd into her perfect-day bubble.

"I should get her home to bed," she said. "And get myself tucked in, too. Let me round up some of her stuff, and I'll take her from you in just a minute, okay?"

She started at the back of the house with the things Kaylee had brought in her princess backpack for the sleepover—toothbrush, stuffed turtle, change of socks—and worked her way forward, gathering presents as she went. She hoped Justin had room in his schedule soon for those snowboarding lessons. Kaylee was revved up about learning and anxious to get started.

As she consolidated smaller gift bags inside large ones, she heard a sound like a whimper. Was Kaylee having a nightmare? Knowing that the girl often woke up in a blind panic, Elisabeth rounded the corner, planning to take her from Justin, but apparently Kaylee had been able to jolt herself out of the bad dream. Elisabeth's daughter opened her eyes and peeked around, then closed them again. "I love you, Justin," she murmured sleepily. "Don't ever go away."

Elisabeth witnessed with perfect clarity how the blood drained from his face. Thank goodness Kaylee didn't see his appalled expression. He looked like he wanted to drop her on the floor and make a run for the nearest exit.

A sob rose in Elisabeth's chest, and she choked it back. What had she told Lina, that as long as there were no expectations, no one could get hurt? How was she going to stop a six-year-old from developing expectations? Justin himself had encouraged Kaylee's faith in him, making it sound as if he'd be right there every step of the way as she learned to snowboard. But he was just as terrified of committing to another person, letting them depend on him, as he always had been.

Stupid. Elisabeth had tried to convince herself this

would work because she wanted him so badly, because she'd never stopped caring about him. But of course Lina had been right. Actions did have consequences. And this time around, when Justin dropped her and ran from what he was feeling, she wouldn't be the only one devastated. Kaylee desperately needed some security in her young life. Elisabeth had been wrong when she'd thought Steven was the man to provide it. But she'd been equally wrong to think, even for a minute, that Justin could fill that requirement. If Kaylee hadn't been in his lap, he probably would have sprinted out the door already.

No. Elisabeth wasn't going through this again. This time, she wasn't waiting for him to say goodbye first.

JUSTIN ONLY HALF heard Elisabeth when she said she was going to warm up the car. His mind was whirling with everything that had happened—her wanting him to make love to her last night, this unforgettable day with her family, Kaylee's touching yet unnerving devotion to him. It was a lot to take in for a man who, two weeks ago, considered himself footloose and fancy-free.

Was that freedom in jeopardy? Elisabeth and Kaylee had somehow managed to infiltrate not just his daily life, running into them about town and including him in their plans, but also unexpected corners of his existence. Songs on the radio that suddenly made him think of Elisabeth, bites of dessert that left him overwhelmed because she'd thought him worth going through so much trouble. An eccentric little tree that made him think of Kaylee every night when he plugged in the lights.

He jerked himself out of his thoughts when he realized that Elisabeth had returned and was saying her goodbyes to her family. "I'll carry her out for you," he said, nodding to the little girl so trustingly curled up against him. "It only makes sense, I'm headed out, too."

Elisabeth nodded, not meeting his gaze. After they buckled Kaylee into her booster seat, would he finally be able to kiss Elisabeth the way he'd wanted to all evening? He wanted to wish her a merry Christmas in a way that went beyond the mere words that everyone from postal workers to store clerks to strangers used. Truthfully, he didn't have words to capture how he felt about her right now.

It was so still outside, the only sound their footsteps crunching through the snow. There was something magical about the night that he hated to disturb.

Elisabeth got to the car first, opening the door for him, and they worked together to slide the sleeping girl into her seat. Justin was torn. Kaylee's whispered *"Don't go away"* had scared him. That wasn't a promise he could make. Who knew what was going to happen between him and Elisabeth? He had no guarantees. Not to mention, he worked a job that frequently meant injuries and, every so often, fatalities. Hearing how attached the girl already was to him, he wondered if distance might not be best for both of them. Yet on the other hand, he could vividly recall her excitement when she'd unwrapped the new snowboard, and he couldn't wait to teach her how to handle it, to watch her confidence grow and her skills blossom.

"I have a full day on the mountain tomorrow and Friday," he told Elisabeth as she closed the car's back door. He was making up for his short schedules yesterday and today with long shifts over the weekend. "I don't know when I'll be able to get together with her."

"I'm not sure you should," she said quietly.

At first, he thought he'd misheard. But he began slowly absorbing telltale details, her rigid posture, the way she was looking in his general direction but not quite meeting his eyes. "Beth, is something wrong?"

"Yes. *I* was wrong. I wanted you so badly that I let it sway my thinking. And I wanted you to have some mythical perfect Christmas, as if that would somehow fix it all. Justin, we shouldn't see each other anymore. Not romantically and not even casually if we can help it. I know that, in a confined space like Cielo Peak, occasional run-ins are bound to happen, but if we—"

"Stop! Just stop. Back up, because you lost me somewhere. What happened to everything you said last night?" He was angry at her hypocrisy. He'd thought things were going so well, which was always the trap. Buying into that illusion that you could be happy and that everything was right with the world. "You said you wanted to be with me, that we could just live in the moment? You lied to me."

"Not intentionally. I was lying to myself, trying to give you the space you needed and still hold on to you. It doesn't work like that. It *shouldn't* work like that." She jammed her hands in her coat pockets. "This is me admitting defeat, taking a page out of the Justin Cade playbook. You're the one who believes getting too close to anyone is an invitation for disaster, and I've decided you're right. So I'm backing off before anyone gets too close. You, me *or* Kaylee. Goodbye, Justin."

She stretched up on tiptoe as if to kiss him farewell, but he jerked away. "Don't do this," he said. "Not now. It *was* a perfect Christmas, and I…"

"The holiday's almost over. People will start taking down decorations, throwing out the cards. Visitors will return home. Reality will creep back in. And this is our reality." She was so calm as she spoke, not even teary, but he knew her better than that. He knew how deep her emotions ran beneath the surface, and he didn't believe for a moment that this was what she wanted.

"We can try," he told her. There was a note in his voice that came too close to begging, and he hated it. Why was he trying to convince her to invest in something he wasn't even sure he could offer?

Because the alternative—letting her go—was unacceptable.

She walked away from him, toward the driver's side, and he chased after her, racking his brain for something he could say to stop her.

You know *what to say.* But the words wouldn't come. He'd conditioned himself so thoroughly not to go there, not to expose himself like that, not to invite loss and pain. "Beth. Please." He resented her for making him ask like this, for damaging his pride.

She climbed into the car, shooting him a pitying look. "Do you remember what you said to Kaylee about her sickening ice cream choices? You congratulated her on being brave enough to try new things. But sometimes, bravery is just the opposite. It's not bouncing from one shiny new thing to the next, it's having the nerve to commit to *one* thing and fight for it. And you're not there yet. Maybe you never will be. For Kaylee's sake—and, I'll admit it, for my own heart's sake—I can't wait around to find out."

Chapter Thirteen

In the days following Christmas, Justin took every shift he could get on the mountain. When individual patrollers needed to change their schedules, it was his or her responsibility to try to arrange coverage before going to the Hill Captain. So many people wanted to make the most of their time with their children before school resumed or with out-of-town guests who hadn't gone home yet. Justin was happy to sub for them all. He worked openings, he worked daily runs, he worked evening patrol, he supervised chairlift evac drills.

Through it all, he ignored Arden's calls and the fact that Elisabeth *hadn't* called. His sister was relentless. She'd left a message the morning of the twenty-sixth wanting details of his Christmas with the Donnellys, followed by another message inviting him and Elisabeth to a New Year's Eve party. Then she apparently spoke to Colin. Justin had already told his temporary roommate that the subject of Elisabeth Donnelly was now closed. Permanently. He must have repeated that to their sister, because she went into a voice-mail-leaving frenzy.

"You have to call me," one message instructed.

"Elisabeth says she doesn't want to talk about it, and Colin says you're even less fun to be around than he is. I know you must have screwed up somehow. If you'd just tell me what happened, I could help you fix it."

No, she couldn't. She couldn't go back in time and change the events that had shaped him, couldn't alter who he fundamentally was. He let his voice mailbox fill up and stopped listening to the recordings.

But his carefully constructed plan of avoiding his problems, and his siblings, couldn't last forever. His supervisor called him in after lunch on Sunday to discuss the number of consecutive shifts Justin had worked.

"We appreciate the extra help during the busy season, son, but safety is our priority. Go home and get some rest before you burn out."

Rest? With Arden stalking him and even Colin making cracks about his disposition? Justin headed for Peak's Pints, where he kept his eyes glued on the football game playing over the bar and didn't make eye contact with a soul.

An hour later, his brother sat on the stool next to him. "Trey Grainger told me he thought I'd find you here. What are we drinking?"

"*We* aren't drinking anything." Justin had ordered a beer when he first sat down but had barely touched it. He wasn't thirsty, and he wasn't in the mood to socialize. In retrospect, perhaps a bar was the wrong place to be. But everything felt wrong now. When he inhaled, the air in his lungs felt wrong, like it was made out of sharp bits that lacerated his insides.

Colin signaled the bartender and got a shot of tequila. Then he looked at Justin. "You're being childish, refusing to tell us about it like that somehow means it didn't happen. Whatever 'it' is, trust me, it happened."

"The girl I wasn't dating dumped me. Which I didn't even realize was possible. She called me a coward. Which I am."

"Did you remind her of the many death-defying acts you've performed on the job? Cades aren't cowards."

Justin spun around on his stool, looking for a fight. "Oh, really? We're not cowards? This from the man who ran away from his life—his family, his job, his home? I ran from Elisabeth's love once before, and now she doesn't trust that I won't do it again. Of the three Cade siblings, Arden's the only one of us with guts. How she found the courage to pursue happiness after the damaged two of us raised her, I'll never know."

Colin grabbed him by the collar of his shirt. "I pursued happiness—and by God I found it. I loved my wife and son, would have died for them. I'm not running, I'm mourning. And as you know nothing about what I've been through, I suggest you shut the hell up."

Ashamed, Justin looked away from his brother, staring instead at his own reflection behind the bottles of liquor on the bar. The man in the mirror was confused. All he'd wanted to do was have fun, ski a lot, help people out and stay off love's radar. It had been a foolproof plan to protect himself, so why was he sitting here now in so much pain? How had it gone wrong?

Sounding calmer and less likely to break a bottle of whisky over Justin's head, his brother asked, "Do you love her?"

Justin sighed. "Not voluntarily."

Colin shot him a disgusted look. "I hope you weren't dumb enough to say it that way to her."

"I didn't say it at all." Couldn't. "After what you've suffered, I'd think you would understand better than anyone. Is the risk really worth it?"

"Hell, yes. Those years I had with Natalie? They were the best of my life. You don't think I'd give anything for another day with her? Another hour? You're talking about us like we're the same, but the woman I loved was *taken* from me. You were just too chicken to hold on to the one you loved."

With those words of brotherly advice, he stood, threw a ten on the bar and announced. "I'm staying with Arden for the rest of this visit. I can't be around this much stupidity—it may be catching. Call us when you pull your head out of your butt, and we'll help you figure out how to win her back."

With Colin out of the house, Justin's place was too quiet, giving him too much space and time to think. On Sunday night, he broke down and called Elisabeth's cell phone. He had no idea what he intended to say to her, but he needed to hear her voice. When she didn't pick up, he thought about all those shifts he'd worked on the mountain. Was it possible she was similarly burying herself in work?

He called the lodge, and Patti Donnelly answered. "I'm sorry, but she doesn't want to talk to you. Don't call here again."

"Can you at least tell her I miss her?" he coaxed.

She sighed heavily into the phone. "I rooted for you, you know. The first time she brought you home,

I could see it, the light in her eyes. When you broke up, I doubted my judgment for weeks. Then it was like fate brought you back together for a second chance. Do you know how rare that is, a second chance in life to atone for your sins and make better choices? But you blew it. Again."

After she hung up on him, he told himself that at least he'd tried. He'd pleaded with Elisabeth on Christmas not to walk away, he'd appealed to Mrs. Donnelly to help him get through to her daughter. To hell with it. He didn't need these stubborn women jerking him around.

But by ten o'clock, he was pacing his kitchen, listening to Lina Donnelly's cell phone ring.

"What do *you* want?" she answered. "I'm not supposed to be talking to you."

"You owe me," he said. "You dragged me into the middle of her life, wanted me to convince her that Steven was a mistake. Now you have to help me convince her that I'm not one."

Something he'd said gave her pause. He'd expected immediate argument, but Lina was uncharacteristically silent. Then, "She knows you're not a mistake. She said as much, point-blank. But she also knows you're not ready for the kind of commitment she and Kaylee deserve. Don't toy with them, Justin. Love her or let her go." Then she disconnected.

Hell. Only one thing to do now. He hadn't wanted it to come to this, but having failed on his own, he was going to have to call in the big guns. Slumping into a chair at the table, trying not to think about the afternoon he and Kaylee had spent here, laughing and making ugly Christmas ornaments, he dialed his sister's number.

IT WAS NEW YEAR'S EVE, a time that symbolized kicking old habits and starting a new life. Justin was ready. He knew what he wanted that life to be and who he wanted in it.

He'd done as Kaylee had asked—he'd hung her drawing on his refrigerator and every time he saw it, his purpose grew clearer. That was a picture of a family, *his* family. As a patroller, there were myriad situations that required risk assessment. And having assessed this situation, he'd concluded that the risks were worth it. He loved Elisabeth, he always had. It was why he'd run from their relationship in the past, but Mrs. Donnelly was right. Only a fool would throw away this second chance at happiness.

Or, technically, third, if he could get Elisabeth to give it to him.

He buttoned up his dress shirt and slid on a blazer. Arden had heard through a friend of a friend where Lina would be celebrating tonight. Best-case scenario was that Lina would drag Elisabeth out with her, and Justin would have a chance to talk to her face-to-face. The Cade charm worked a lot better in person. But he also had a Plan B, and his sister had armed him with visual aids to plead his case.

Cielo Peak's "historic downtown" consisted of one street, home to some stately buildings like the courthouse and funkier venues like an independently owned art gallery. There was a special showing open to the public tonight and a party on the gallery's top floor. Justin thought that giving people drinks all night and then convincing them they simply had to have a six-hundred-dollar oil painting titled *Fuchsia Regrets* was a brilliant marketing strategy.

He wound his way through the crowd, feeling hopeful when he spotted Nicole Lewis, an eye-catching beacon in a yellow-and-red column dress. Did that mean Beth was here, too? Mentally crossing his fingers, he made his way toward her, but she didn't even let him get a word out before holding up her hand in the universally recognized sign for *halt, stop right there.*

"I am here on a date," she said. "He'll be back with our drinks any moment, and I don't want you getting your bad romance karma on me. I really like this one. So, scoot."

"Fair enough." He gave her the same imploring look that had once convinced a first year geometry teacher to bump his D to a C so he could stay on the ski team. He hadn't resorted to such cheap tricks in years, but for Elisabeth, he was shameless. "Will you at least tell me if you've seen Lina here tonight?"

Nicole sighed. "It would be easier to say no to you if you didn't have those eyes. Check the east gallery."

"You're an angel." He winked at her. "Good luck with your date."

He headed in the direction she'd pointed him in and nearly collided with Lina in the corridor. "Just the beautiful Donnelly twin I was looking for," he said. "Unless of course your even more beautiful sister is *also* here?"

"Dude. Did you just call me the ugly Donnelly twin?"

"There are no ugly Donnellys." He took her by the elbow and gently but inexorably tugged her toward a bench in the gallery. The light was nice and bright in here which suited his purposes. "I need to show you something, Lina. It'll just take a second of your time, then you can get back to the party."

He reached into his jacket and pulled out the envelope of pictures Arden had given him. The one of Steven and Elisabeth so close together made his lip curl. How had Steven let her go so easily, simply walked away from her as if his new life in California wasn't worth giving her a single backward glance? *You're one to judge. You didn't just walk away. Last time around, you sprinted.*

"Here's your sister with the guy she briefly considered marrying."

"I don't need the recap, bozo. I was there."

"Right. Just do me a favor and really look at the picture. She's smiling, but does she look happy?"

Lina obligingly took the photo from him, and when she shook her head in defeat, hope soared through him.

"Now here's one Arden took of me and Elisabeth on Christmas Eve. Next to the drawing Kaylee gave me, it's my favorite picture in the world."

He and Elisabeth hadn't posed for the photo. He hadn't even known Arden took it until afterward, when she gave it to him. He and Elisabeth had been teasing each other, trash-talking each other's dance moves after some story Garrett told about a long-ago prom. Justin and Elisabeth weren't touching in the frame, but they stood very close together, her with her hands planted on her hips, her head tilted up, green fire in her eyes and a sassy smile on her face.

He was looking down at her, laughing, more at home with her than he was anywhere in the world. Including on the mountain.

He asked his question again, his voice low, feeling as if his entire world hinged on Lina's answer. "Does she look happy?"

"Yeah. Yes, okay? She looked very happy. But this is not how she looked after you dumped her over the summer while she was in the middle of losing her best friend."

"I know. I'm not proud of how I bailed on her, but watching her lose someone she loved, to the same disease that took my mom... I don't want to make excuses. I want to make it up to her. Will you help me?"

She stood, pacing in the small space, her skyscraper heels clicking on the floor. "She was pretty clear when she said she didn't want me talking to you."

He rose. "You can tell me no tonight, but that doesn't mean I won't wear you down eventually. 'I don't think you're prepared for how focused I am when I want something. This is my hometown, too,'" he quoted. "'We could run into each other a *lot*.'"

She stopped, dumbfounded, then burst out laughing. "That's not fair. How am I supposed to argue with my own words?"

His heart raced. "Does that mean you'll help me?"

"This one time, against my better judgment. But Justin? Do not screw it up."

ELISABETH TUCKED THE to-go container under her arm and dug through the pocket of her trench coat for the keys. Her sister had phoned the lodge half an hour ago asking if Elisabeth, who was coming to town anyway to get Kaylee off the school bus, would bring her some of Chef Bates's famous garlic soup.

"I haven't eaten all day," Lina had said, moaning dramatically. "And that soup is the only thing that sounds good."

Elisabeth had been surprised when her sister called in sick that morning. Javier had mentioned seeing Lina and a friend at a movie last night and that she'd seemed just fine. But it was flu season, and these things could come on suddenly.

She unlocked the door to her sister's house. Technically, the place belonged to one of Lina's former boyfriends, but she was subletting from him while his band toured abroad. They were big in Germany.

"Lina? It's me. Do you want me to bring you a bowl of soup now, or just leave it in the microwave?" She went straight to the kitchen, listening for instructions on what to do next.

But when she got there, the sight of Justin standing at the center of the room shook her so badly she almost dropped the soup.

"Hi, Beth."

She frowned. "When I find my sister, I am going to become an only child."

"I can help you with her location. She went to pick up Kaylee from the bus, so we'd have time to talk."

No. This wasn't fair! She'd done the responsible, adult thing. Justin Cade was the most tempting man she'd ever known, the sexiest and, when he wanted to be, the most fun. Walking away from him had been damn difficult but she'd done it because she thought it was best for her and for Kaylee. Having survived that test, why was she being challenged now? Why was the man whose every relationship came with an expiration date suddenly giving her the full-court press?

"We don't have anything to talk about," she said, trying to keep the tremor out of her voice. She was not going to cry in front of him. She set the soup on the table, turning away from those tropical eyes and any argument he might try to make.

"What about ice cream?" he asked.

Okay...that, she hadn't expected. "Come again?"

"Ice cream. You said I didn't have the nerve to commit to just one flavor." He crossed the kitchen to the stainless steel refrigerator, opening the freezer side. It was packed solid with, as far as she could tell, nothing but peppermint ice cream. "Well, I'm committing. That's not all of it, either," he said matter-of-factly. "I bought out all the peppermint ice cream in town. There are a few more gallons at my place and your folks'—"

"My *parents* are in on this?" She pressed a hand to her chest, feeling utterly betrayed.

"Elisabeth, I've spent a week and a half working to convince the most important people in your life of how much I love you. That I can be counted on to be there for you and Kaylee, no matter what."

Her knees almost buckled. In her wildest dreams, she never thought she'd actually hear him say it. Tears blurred her vision. "Y-you love me?"

"With all my heart." His voice broke, and he

stopped, looking away in an attempt to compose himself. She adored him for that. Justin Cade had never broken a sweat for a woman, never had to work for one.

"Please tell me that it's not too late," he said, taking a step toward her. "That there's still a chance you could love me?"

She waited until he was close enough to touch to launch herself into his arms. "I never stopped."

His lips took hers in a soul-shaking kiss. If he'd opened with this, he wouldn't have needed the words because his feelings were so clear. No one had ever kissed her with this much passion, and within moments she was breathless with need.

He gave a small growl of protest when she stepped backward, out of his embrace. She reached for the belt of her jacket and let her coat fall to the floor. Then she reached for the top button of her blouse. "You say Lina has Kaylee and we have time?"

In answer, he swept her into his arms and began carrying her toward the stairs. "Plenty of time."

Between kisses, she couldn't help tease, "You know the ice cream thing was insane, right? What are we going to do with all of that?"

"I was going for 'grand romantic gesture' but if insane works... Hold on." He set her upright, then dashed back into the kitchen. He returned with a small single-sized container of gourmet peppermint and a spoon. "I can think of a few places I'd like to lick this off. As for the rest of it, maybe instead of throwing an engagement party like a normal couple, we can have an ice cream social."

Engagement? Her jaw dropped. "Did you just ask me to marry you?"

"Did I? Damn. I had planned to wait until you were shaking with desire and willing to agree to something as crazy as life with me."

She cupped his face, touched that he was willing to take such a leap of faith. "I know I've talked about being ready to settle down, but I'm not trying to rush you. I realize a step this big must scare the hell out of you. You don't have to put a ring on my finger just to hold on to me."

He pulled her into his arms. "Beth, nothing in this world is as scary as not being with you. Everything else we'll handle. Together."

WHEN JUSTIN WALKED into the lodge to pick up Kaylee for their weekly snowboarding lesson, he was struck by the sense of family. For so long, his only family had been his brother and sister. Now Colin was back on the road, and Arden had moved her things to the Double F Ranch. But Justin had never been less lonely in his life. Since his engagement to Elisabeth, the Donnellys had all but adopted him. Nicole and Lina kept coming to him for advice on men. The loyal employees at the lodge, even Javier, were downright adoring as long as he kept their Elisabeth happy. Which was his plan, from now until forever.

Kaylee, who was sitting next to Elisabeth at the reception desk and drawing, spotted him first. "Justin! I have to get my jacket. I'll be quick like a bunny." But she paused, giving him a stern look. "No kissing, Mom.

It's okay at home but it's gross when you're where everyone can see you."

He heard Elisabeth's soft gasp, noticed the tremor in her fingers she tried to hide by clenching her fists. Though she didn't embarrass Kaylee by making a big deal over it, he knew it was the first time the girl had called her Mom. He applauded the title—Elisabeth had more than earned it.

When Kaylee was out of earshot, he said, "That's quite a daughter you're raising."

"*We're* raising. Don't forget, you've signed on for this, too."

Joy bloomed within him, making it difficult to breathe. "So am I allowed to kiss you hello, or is she right? Will we sicken the entire population?"

"I think we do that anyway. I can't stop smiling." But in contradiction to her words, she scowled suddenly.

He turned around, hoping there was something behind him that had caused that expression and not anything he'd done. A steel-haired woman in a leopard-print sweater stood at the restaurant podium, lambasting Javier about something.

"She's done nothing but complain since she got here," Elisabeth whispered. "She pitched a fit last night to get Javier to make an exception to our reservation policy, but then she and her large group made other plans at the last minute. Now she expects him to squeeze in fifteen people tonight!"

"Want me to toss her out in the snow?" he offered. "I'm still trying to suck up to Javier."

She laughed. "Wouldn't it just be easier to distract her with your charm and get Javier off the hook? Charming women is supposed to be your specialty."

"Nope." He leaned across the reception desk to give her a slow, languid kiss. He didn't care who saw them. He wanted the world to know how he felt about this woman and how committed he was to her. "My specialty is loving you."

* * * * *

Look for HER COWBOY HERO, the last book in Tanya Michaels's COLORADO CADES *trilogy, in June 2014!*

#1481 HER CALLAHAN FAMILY MAN

Callahan Cowboys

Tina Leonard

When Jace Callahan and Sawyer Cash engaged in their secretive affair, neither of them anticipated an unplanned pregnancy. Jace wants to seal the deal with a quickie marriage...but it turns out he has a very reluctant bride!

#1482 MARRYING THE COWBOY

Blue Falls, Texas

Trish Milburn

When a tornado rips through Blue Falls, good friends Elissa Mason and Pete Kayne find themselves sharing a house. Suddenly Elissa is thinking about her *pal* in a whole new way....

#1483 THE SURPRISE HOLIDAY DAD

Safe Harbor Medical

Jacqueline Diamond

Adrienne Cavill delivers other women's babies, but can't have one of her own. Now she may lose the nephew she's raising, and her heart, to his long-absent father, Wade Hunter. Unless the two of them can come up with a different arrangement?

#1484 RANCHER AT RISK

Barbara White Daille

Ryan Molloy's job is running his boss's ranch, so he doesn't have time to babysit Lianne Ward. She's there to establish a boys' camp—and definitely doesn't need Ryan looking over her shoulder every minute!

———

REQUEST YOUR FREE BOOKS!
2 FREE NOVELS PLUS 2 FREE GIFTS!

HARLEQUIN®

American ★ Romance®

LOVE, HOME & HAPPINESS

YES! Please send me 2 FREE Harlequin® American Romance® novels and my 2 FREE gifts (gifts are worth about $10). After receiving them, if I don't wish to receive any more books, I can return the shipping statement marked "cancel." If I don't cancel, I will receive 4 brand-new novels every month and be billed just $4.74 per book in the U.S. or $5.24 per book in Canada. That's a savings of at least 14% off the cover price! It's quite a bargain! Shipping and handling is just 50¢ per book in the U.S. and 75¢ per book in Canada.* I understand that accepting the 2 free books and gifts places me under no obligation to buy anything. I can always return a shipment and cancel at any time. Even if I never buy another book, the two free books and gifts are mine to keep forever.

154/354 HDN F4YN

Name	(PLEASE PRINT)
Address	Apt. #
City	State/Prov.	Zip/Postal Code

Signature (if under 18, a parent or guardian must sign)

Mail to the **Harlequin® Reader Service:**
IN U.S.A.: P.O. Box 1867, Buffalo, NY 14240-1867
IN CANADA: P.O. Box 609, Fort Erie, Ontario L2A 5X3

Want to try two free books from another line?
Call 1-800-873-8635 or visit www.ReaderService.com.

* Terms and prices subject to change without notice. Prices do not include applicable taxes. Sales tax applicable in N.Y. Canadian residents will be charged applicable taxes. Offer not valid in Quebec. This offer is limited to one order per household. Not valid for current subscribers to Harlequin American Romance books. All orders subject to credit approval. Credit or debit balances in a customer's account(s) may be offset by any other outstanding balance owed by or to the customer. Please allow 4 to 6 weeks for delivery. Offer available while quantities last.

Your Privacy—The Harlequin® Reader Service is committed to protecting your privacy. Our Privacy Policy is available online at www.ReaderService.com or upon request from the Harlequin Reader Service.

We make a portion of our mailing list available to reputable third parties that offer products we believe may interest you. If you prefer that we not exchange your name with third parties, or if you wish to clarify or modify your communication preferences, please visit us at www.ReaderService.com/consumerchoice or write to us at Harlequin Reader Service Preference Service, P.O. Box 9062, Buffalo, NY 14269. Include your complete name and address.

HAR13R

*Their families may be rivals, but Jace Callahan
just can't stay away from Sawyer Cash!*

Jace Callahan appeared to be locked in place, thunderstruck. What had him completely poleaxed was that the little darling who had such spunk was quite clearly as pregnant as a busy bunny in spring.

She made no effort to hide it in a curve-hugging hot pink dress with long sleeves and a high waist. Taupe boots adorned her feet, and she looked sexy as a goddess, but for the glare she wore just for him.

A pregnant Sawyer Cash was a thorny issue, especially since she was the niece of their Rancho Diablo neighbor, Storm Cash. The Callahans didn't quite trust Storm, in spite of the fact that they'd hired Sawyer on to bodyguard the Callahan kinder.

But then Sawyer had simply vanished off the face of the earth, leaving only a note of resignation behind. No forwarding address, a slight that he'd known was directed at him.

Jace knew this because for the past year he and Sawyer had had "a thing," a secret they'd worked hard to keep completely concealed from everyone.

He'd missed sleeping with her these past many months she'd elected to vacate Rancho Diablo with no forwarding address. Standing here looking at her brought all the familiar desire back like a screaming banshee.

Yet clearly they had a problem. Best to face facts right up front. "Is that why you went away from Rancho Diablo?" he asked, pointing to her tummy.

She raised her chin. "It won't surprise me if you back out, Jace. You were never one for commitment."

Commitment, his boot. Of his six siblings, consisting of one sister and five brothers, he'd been the one who'd most longed to settle down.

He gazed at her stomach again, impressed by the righteous size to which she'd grown in the short months since he'd last seen her—and slept with her.

He wished he could drag her to his bed right now.

"I'm your prize, beautiful," he said with a grin. "No worries about that."

Look for HER CALLAHAN FAMILY MAN,
by USA TODAY bestselling author Tina Leonard
next month, from Harlequin® American Romance®.

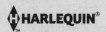
HARLEQUIN®

American Romance®

Guess who's coming home for Christmas…

Dr. Adrienne Cavill couldn't love her nephew more if he were her own child. And no deadbeat dad is going to claim the little boy she's practically raised.

Wade Hunter's past and future await the detective turned P.I. He missed five years of his son's life, and nothing's chasing him away this time. That includes the pretty doctor who's giving his child everything—except the father he needs.

Now that she knows the reasons why he left, how can Adrienne keep the rugged ex-cop from his son—or from her, for that matter? Will Christmas bring Adrienne the family she never thought she could have?

The Surprise Holiday Dad
by JACQUELINE DIAMOND

**Available January 2014,
from Harlequin® American Romance®.**

www.Harlequin.com

HAR75504

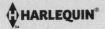

American Romance®

A fresh start

After the loss of his family in a tragic accident,
Ryan Malloy has been given one last chance to change
his life. His boss sends him to Flagman's Folly,
New Mexico, to run his ranch, but unfortunately, Ryan's
troubled attitude lands him in hot water with the ranch's
gutsy project manager, Lianne Ward.

Deaf since birth, Lianne has never let her disability
define her. But she's yet to meet a man who treats her as
an equal. Ryan seems different…that is, when they're not
butting heads.

Forced to work together, Lianne and Ryan discover an
unexpected attraction beneath their quarreling. But will
Ryan's painful past drive them apart…permanently?

Rancher At Risk
by BARBARA WHITE DAILLE

**Available January 2014,
from Harlequin® American Romance®.**